By the same author

Hell Paso

Shadow Peak

Drifter Reason Conant is sheltering in a ca
midwinter storm when a stranger bursts in on
kills him in self-defence. Then he finds that
has a bullet wound, his saddlebags contain a
money but no provisions, and his canteen is
someone had evidently not wanted the man
the wild.

Reason's hunch that trouble is close by
he is captured by Sheriff Kramer and his poss
of murdering the local newspaper edito
newspaperman's daughter Annie suspects tha
seems when she finds evidence that her father
to reveal corruption among local officials – i
Kramer. And in the mean time, Reason Cona
hanged for a murder he did not commit.

Shadow Peak

Matt Cole

A Black Horse Western
ROBERT HALE

ISBN 978-0-7198-2016-8

The Crowood Press
The Stable Block
Crowood Lane
Ramsbury
Marlborough
Wiltshire SN8 2HR

www.crowood.com

Robert Hale is an imprint
of The Crowood Press

Typeset by Catherine Williams, Knebworth

Printed and bound in Great Britain by
CPI Antony Rowe, Chippenham and Eastbourne

CHAPTER 1

The sky had been progressively gloomy with leaden-coloured clouds, until, when near sunset, it was one huge dark-blue mass of rolling darkness: the wind had unexpectedly calmed and an unnatural lull, which so surely heralds a storm in these stormy regions, succeeded.

The peaks of the Teton Range; regal and imposing as they stood some seven thousand feet above the valley floor, casting their shadows over all below them.

The ravens were winging their way towards the shelter of the timber, and the coyote was seen trotting quickly to cover, conscious of the coming storm.

The black, menacing clouds seemed gradually to descend until they caressed the earth, and already the distant mountains were hidden to their very bases. A hollow susurrating swept through the bottom, but as yet not a branch stirred by wind; and the huge cottonwoods, with their leafless limbs, loomed like a line of ghosts through the heavy gloom. Knowing but too well what was coming, the drifter turned his horse towards the timber, which was about two miles distant. With pointed ears, and actually shuddering with fright, the horse was as eager as he was to shelter; but, before they had proceeded a third of the distance, with a deafening roar the tempest broke upon them. The clouds opened and the enormous hailstones, beating on Reason's unprotected head and face, almost stunned him. In an instant his hunting shirt was soaked, and as instantly frozen hard; his horse was a mass of icicles. Jumping off his mount – for to ride was nearly impossible – he tore off the saddle blanket and covered his head. The animal, blinded with the sleet, its eyes actually with ice, turned its sterns to the storm, and, blown before it, made for cover. All his exertions to drive the animal to the shelter of the timber were useless. It was impossible to face the blizzard, which now brought with it clouds of driving snow; and perfect darkness soon set in.

Still the mount kept on, and the drifter was determined not to leave the animal, following, or rather being blown after it. His blanket, frozen stiff like a board, required all the strength of his numbed fingers to prevent it being carried away, and although it was no protection against the intense cold, he knew it would in some degree shelter him at night from the snow. In half an hour the ground was covered on the bare trail to the depth of several feet, and through this he floundered for a long time before the horse stopped. The trail was as bare as a lake, but one little tuft of greasewood bushes presented itself and here, turning from the storm, man and horse suddenly stopped and remained perfectly still. In vain he again attempted to turn towards the timber; huddled together, the horse would not move an inch and exhausted himself, seeing nothing before him but, as he thought, certain death, he sank down immediately behind the horse, and, covering his head with the blanket, crouched like a ball in the snow.

He would have started himself for the timber but it was pitch black, the wind drove clouds of frozen snow into his face, and the horse had so turned about in the trail that it was impossible to know the direction to take. Although he had some sense of direction about him, this was lost in the swirling cold and darkness. Even if he had reached the timber, his situation would have been scarcely improved, for the trees were scattered wide about over a narrow space and consequently afforded but little shelter. Even if the drifter had succeeded in finding firewood – by no means an easy task at any time, and still more difficult now that the ground was covered with three feet of snow – he was utterly unable to use his flint and steel to procure a light, since his fingers were like pieces of stone, and entirely without feeling.

He would not attempt to describe the way the wind roared over the trail that night, how the snow drove before it, covering Reason and his poor mount partly and how he lay there, feeling the blood freezing in his veins, his bones petrifying with icy blasts which seemed to pierce them. How for hours he remained with his head on his knees, the snow pressing it down like a weight of lead, expecting every instant to drop into a sleep from which it would be impossible to wake. How every now and then the horse would whimper aloud and fall down upon the snow, and then again struggle on to its legs. How all night long the piercing howl of wolves was borne upon the wind, which never for an instant abated its violence. Reason had passed many nights alone in the wilderness, and in a solitary camp had listened to the roaring upon

7

him with perfect unconcern, but this night threw all his former experiences into the shade, and was marked with the blackest of stones in the letters of his journeys.

Once, late in the night, by keeping his hands buried in the breast of his hunting shirt and sheepskin-lined canvas jacket, he succeeded in restoring sufficient feeling into them to be able to strike a light. Fortuitously his pipe, which was made out of a huge piece of cottonwood bark, and capable of containing at least twelve ordinary pipe-fulls, was filled with tobacco to the brim and this he did believe kept him alive during the night, for he smoked and smoked until the pipe itself caught fire, and burned completely to the stem.

He was sinking into a pensive apathy when the horse began to shake itself and sneeze and snort, which Reason hailed as a good sign; a sign that they were still alive. The drifter attempted to lift his head and take a view of the weather. When with great difficulty he raised his head, all appeared dark as pitch, and it did not at first occur to him that he was buried deep in snow. But when he thrust his arm above a hole was thus made, through which he saw stars shining in the sky and the clouds fast clearing away. Making a sudden attempt to straighten his almost petrified back and limbs, the drifter rose but, unable to stand, fell forward in the snow, frightening the horse, which immediately started away. When he gained his legs he found that day was just breaking, a long grey line of light appearing over the belt of timber on the creek, and the clouds gradually rising from the east, allowing the stars to peep from patches of blue sky. Following the horse as soon as he gained the use of his limbs, and taking a last look at the perfect cave he had been trying to reach, he found he was in the timber and jumping on the horse, galloped back towards the cave, his original destination, his stomach groaning loudly from hunger pangs.

CHAPTER 2

A man could die out here; that much he had learned from the prior night's storm.

That was not the first time the thought had occurred to Reason Conant as he eased his weary mount along the narrow, snow-packed mountain trail.

He crossed the stream below the pool, stepping agilely from stone to stone. Where the hillside touched the water, he dug up a shovelful of snow and dirt into his gold pan. He was always looking for the quick strike; he was not afraid of hard work, but would take good fortune over it.

He hunkered down in his sheepskin-lined canvas jacket and wished he had taken the time to replace the two rawhide ties that had come loose and eventually been lost, some weeks earlier. The icy wind knifed through the openings and found his shivering flesh beneath his woollen shirt and worn undershirt. The long johns he wore were frayed at the knees and his corduroy trousers were not thick enough to keep out the chill. He wore all the socks he owned – three pairs. He could hardly jam his feet into the worn and scuffed half-boots, but at least they were warm. Thick, buckskin mittens hid frozen hands.

He had tied a woollen scarf under his chin and covered the knot on top of his head with his battered old hat to keep his ears and head warm. But his face and mouth were so numb, he could not feel the tip of his nose or his lips.

He squatted down, holding the pan in his two hands, and partly immersing it in the stream just outside the entrance to the cave. Then he imparted to the pan a deft circular motion that sent the freezing water and snow sluicing in and out through the dirt, ice and gravel. Occasionally, to expedite matters, especially in this brutal cold, he rested the pan and with his fingers, frozen as there were, raked out large pebbles and pieces of rock.

The contents of the pan diminished rapidly until only fine dirt and the smallest icicles and bits of gravel remained. At this stage he began to work very deliberately and carefully. It was fine washing and if the weather had been better, he may have found something worth his effort.

As it was now the fury of the storm was increasing. The wind howled louder and stronger gusts set him swaying in the saddle of his plodding horse. A man's imagination could so strange things in country like this, Reason thought, squinting at weird, wraith-like shapes flickering across his line of vision. He knew they were jagged rocks or bushes clinging to the steep, eroded sides of the mountains, distorted by swirling drifts of snow. But if a man was not careful, he could easily mistake one of them for some sort of animal or mythical creature looming before him and instinctively wrench the reins the wrong way, sending his horse plunging into space.

On the contrary, Reason Conant was used to the high country. He had been drifting around it for several years, going from job to job, dodging a little trouble occasionally, bending the law here and there, but managing to survive. He was an easy-going man, not too proud to bend his back to any job that paid honest dollars. Once in a while, he threw a wide loop, when his pockets were empty and his belly growling, but not too often. And when he did, he only took cattle to get himself a grubstake to see him through to the next country, where there might be work available.

That was why he had gotten himself caught on this high trail in the midst of a storm.

Things had been tough lately. He had not had a square meal for four days when he had met up with two hard cases who were preparing to run off some steers from a big ranch – the same one that had, earlier, thrown Reason off. He did not mind any rancher refusing work, for usually they gave him a meal and sometimes a bunk before sending him on his way. But this particular ranch had been run by a son of a bitch who had not only refused Reason work, but had turned loose his ramrod and two other tough rannies on him. They had worked him over before running him off. He had been thinking about getting even when he had chanced on the hard cases. Together, they had rustled twenty prime beeves and sold them to a shifty-eyed man in the Tetons who had paid about three cents in the dollar. It had been enough to buy Reason a saddlebag full of grub and some oats for his horse.

He had parted company with the hard cases and didn't know that, later, they had been picked up by the

12

county law and charged with rustling.

Reason Conant was also unaware that these same men, after being beaten and harassed by the rancher, had given his description to the sheriff who had circulated it throughout the whole of Utah and surrounding areas.

Even if he had known he might be picked up on a rustling charge, it would not have bothered Reason Conant right then. He was too intent on finding shelter to worry about anything else.

By now, he figured, he should be coming to flat ground – a ledge he had spotted earlier, before the snow had begun to fall heavily. He knew he was on the right trail, but it seemed a hell of a long time since he had left the canyon below and started up here. Of course, he should have waited out the storm below, instead of trying to go up and over at this time of year. But Reason Conant had figured to save time and hopefully to reach East Valley City, under the gloom of Shadow Peak in the Teton Mountains, not long after nightfall and so find some hot grub and a warm bed for the night.

It had been a mistake, obviously, but he had not expected a storm to blow up so swiftly. Now it was full dark and he was in one hell of a dangerous position. If the horse took one false step he would be finished. The snow was coming in thick, blinding swirls now, and he could not see more than a few feet in front of him. He hoped the horse could see the trail.

Suddenly, the animal started to whinny frantically, but the sound was cut short. Reason instinctively grabbed at the saddle horn and, even as he felt it begin to tilt wildly, cursed and started to kick his feet free of the stirrups. But then again, due to the cold, the leather of his boots was stiff and unyielding and would not free easily. He yelled as he felt the horse starting to go, then the white world of the snowstorm titled and spun eerily and he felt the rush of numbing, ice cold air as he plunged down through space, knowing with heart-hammering certainty that the horse had stepped off the mountain into oblivion.

The storm was not so cruel in East Valley City. Here the hills gave the small cow town some protection, cushioning the biting winds as they swept down from the high country. Lower foothills and the heavy timber also helped kill the blizzard winds, and by the time they reached the town, they were little more than annoying. This wasn't to say, of course, that snowstorms did not swirl through the town and make life miserable for anybody who happened to be abroad.

Gus Lannan could attest to that. He shivered as he pulled his fur-lined canvas jacket tighter about his neck, turning up the collar and burrowing his head down. The brim of his hat was tugged low over his eyes and the tip of his nose felt as if it would snap clean off if he touched it. He hated high country winters and if the pay offered for this job had not been so blamed good, he would not have come to this godforsaken town to begin with.

But, with the law spreading like a plague throughout the West these days, a man of Lannan's calling had to go where the jobs were. And it seemed that not too many people wanted a paid killer and gunfighter nowadays. So, when he received the mysterious letter calling him to East Valley City and offering big money, Lannan had saddled up and ridden in, despite the wintry weather. He would sure be glad to hit the sack tonight, he told himself, and snuggle down under some warm blankets – maybe with a saloon gal's body alongside him for extra comfort and warmth. The thought excited him and he straightened in the saddle, momentarily ignoring the cold wind as he looked around for the rendezvous point. The letter had said to arrive after dark, but definitely before nine o'clock, and to watch for a man who would call him by name at the steepled, shingle-roofed church on the west side of town. Lannan could see the church spire rearing against the greyness of the lightly swirling snow, so he kneed his mount towards it, right hand loosening one of the rawhide ties of his jacket and pushing the front panel back, so that it caught behind the butt of the holstered gun on his hip.

The icy wind attacked him but Lannan was not taking any chances. Especially not in a strange town where he was meeting a stranger, whose letter had only promised a big deal and enclosed a bare hundred dollars for expenses.

He rode into the churchyard, barely glancing at the tilted, weathered headboards. Snow seemed to spit into his face and he swore as he wiped it from his eyes and mouth. The wind had changed and he ducked his head low, using his hat brim to shield his eyes, as sleet rattled mutedly against the canvas jacket. There was movement by the south corner of the church, to the left of the main door. Lannan's Colt swept up smoothly and the click of the hammer going back to full cock could be heard even above the whine of the wind.

'Call out, feller,' he ordered quietly, reins in his left hand ready to spur his mount away at the first signs of a trap.

'If you're Gus Lannan, you got nothin' to worry about, mister,' a voice replied.

'You leave the worryin' to me. Step out where I can see you,' ordered Lannan.

The man came out from the shadow of the church, hands held shoulder high. He was tall and beneath the bulky winter clothing, Lannan figured he was lean. The man's face was hard to tell the difference, but Gus Lannan could see that it was narrow, iron-jawed, and the nose seemed to jut, throwing a dark shadow across his thin lips. He guessed the man to be in his late twenties, maybe slightly older. There was no weapon in evidence, although the bulge under the flap of his sheep-hide jacket could only be that of the butt of a gun.

'I'm Lannan.' The killer spoke up, not lowering his gun hammer. 'If you're the hombre I'm supposed to meet, you ought to have somethin' for me.'

'I'll have to reach into my jacket for it,' the man said nervously.

'Go ahead, but take it slow and careful,' Lannan replied. 'I'm not one to wait for surprises … I'll shoot first without worryin' about the consequences.'

The man swallowed hard but obeyed, easing a slim oilskin package from his jacket and offering it to Lannan. The gunfighter reached down with his left hand and took it. The gun barrel jerked towards the porch of the church.

'Lie down on your face – arms and legs spread.'

'Like hell!' protested the man. 'There's slush here.'

Gus Lannan walked his horse forward a step. 'OK. I'll just bounce my gun barrel off your head while I check the package.'

'Whoa mister!' the man said, jumping back suddenly. 'No need for that. Look, I'll lock my fingers on top of my head and wrap my legs around the porch post. OK? It's too damn cold to lie down in that slush.'

'All right,' Lannan agreed and watched the man take up his position. When he was satisfied, he lowered his gun hammer and laid the Colt carefully across his thigh while he opened the oilskin and swiftly counted the money inside. He jerked his head up, shadowed face hard. 'There's only half here.'

The nervous man on the porch nodded awkwardly. 'You get the other half when the job's done. I'll be waiting at the end of the lane; I'll show you where with a fresh horse, saddlebags of grub and water canteens. All you gotta do is hit leather and vamoose.'

'You better be there, you understand me, boy?'

'I will. We want this job done proper, which is why we're paying so well.'

Lannan smiled thinly. 'So you ain't the only one in it.'

'That don't concern you none,' the man replied, without heat. 'You just do the job, collect your money and be on your way. Your tracks will be covered in a couple of miles of snow.'

Lannan stiffened. 'What? You mean to tell me that you want the job done tonight?'

The man puckered his brow. 'Hell, yeah! Why would you think I stressed you had to be here by nine o'clock?'

'Man, it's freezin'! I want a warm bunk and a woman for the night. I'll do the job tomorrow,' Lannan countered.

The lean man on the porch shook his head. 'It's got to be tonight. Tomorrow will be too late.'

Lannan thought about it. 'What would you've done if I hadn't showed?'

'I'd have had to do the chore myself, which would have been too risky. We want this hombre gunned down by a complete stranger, and that's you, mister. His death can't be connected with anyone in this town. So you shoot him, then you ransack the place and take the cash box – I'll tell you where it is – and make it look like robbery. Oh! There's a book, too.'

'A book? What the hell ...?' Lannan began to protest.

'It's important. It's black Morocco leather, corners brass bound with a filigreed brass lock. It'll be with the cash box. If not, you'll have to look for it.'

'Uh-uh. There won't be time for any big search. Once I shoot him, I want to get out and away as quick as I can,' Lannan answered.

'Sure, but he's by himself. This storm will deaden the sound of the shot, and, anyway, it's too cold for folk to come out to investigate. There will be time to look for the book.'

'I would have asked for more money if I'd known. In fact, it ain't too late.'

The man shook his head. 'There's no more. We raised every cent we could. That's why we offered so much in the first place, Lannan.'

'Yeah? Well, maybe I'll look you up again. It sounds like you're pullin' a fast one on me; didn't gimme all the details. I don't like this kind of thing bein' sprung on me, mister.'

'Well, hell, mister, I couldn't put all the details in that letter, I didn't know who might get to see it,' the man explained.

'All right. I'm freezin' my ass off sittin' here. Let's go get this lousy job done,' Lannan shot back.

The man untangled himself from the porch post and led the way through the deserted town, where only a few lights burned dully behind drawn drapes. The smell of smoke was heavy and pungent from wood burning in fireplaces. The wind howled mournfully between the buildings. Snow swirled and created brief apparitions in the night. The man leading the way stopped in the mouth of an alley between a grain store and a saddlery shop. He pointed across the wide, slushy street towards a lighted building, where Lannan could see the vague shape of someone moving around behind the misted street-front window.

'That's your man,' the lean stranger declared.

'Hell, a newspaper office. This is getting' worse, amigo. Lots of light, big street-front window. I ain't out of my head with excitement at the prospect, friend.'

The other man shrugged. 'That's it. His name's Clive Burch, but I guess that don't make no never mind to you. He's putting his paper to bed about now.'

'To bed?' Gus Lannan asked.

The man made an impatient gesture. 'Preparing to print it,' he explained shortly. 'He's got a stove going to keep him warm while he sets the type for the paper. That's why the window's misted with the heat. There will be sheets of handwritten copy beside that stove. We want that too, or you can burn it – just as long as it is destroyed. That's what's important.'

Lannan climbed down from his mount stiffly and stared into the wolfish face of the other man. 'You're sure after your money's worth, friend. Now you better have that horse waitin' and the rest of the money, or I don't leave this town till I blow your head off. You git me?'

The man's gaze didn't waver. 'No need for threats, Lannan. We will stick to our bargain. You just do your part and do it well. You will have no complaints.'

As he spoke, the man thrust his hands into his jacket pockets in order to keep them warm. As he did so, the lapels of the jacket moved and Lannan caught a glimpse of something metallic. His Colt whipped up and the barrel bored into the other's belly. As the man's wolfish face paled with shock, Lannan ripped open his jacket, expecting to see the butt of a hideaway gun in a shoulder holster.

He blinked in surprise. It wasn't the butt of a gun he had seen glinting in the dim light.

It was a brass sheriff's badge that was pinned to the man's shirt.

CHAPTER 3

Reason Conant knew he was fortunate to be alive. His jacket had caught on a stubby branch of a lone bush halfway down the slope and was now stretched to its limit. He had banged his head hard on the way down, dislodging his hat, which now hung down his back by the rawhide tie-thong. However, the scarf tied around his face kept his head warm.

His horse was somewhere below, lost in the white swirl of snow. He was sure it was dead for, after his coat had been caught up on the bush, he had heard its crashing passage for a long time before it had finally come to rest. Conant hoped it wasn't too far down, as he knew he was going to have to climb down there, once he freed himself from the bush. He needed the grub in the saddlebags and the canteen of water, as well as his war bag and rifle.

Reason Conant did not intend to be set afoot in this kind of country without food, blankets and a long gun. He knew grizzlies and pumas roamed these hills and a six-gun would be practically useless against either animal. The bears should be hibernating, but he had learned, long ago, that if a man aimed to survive, he didn't take anything for granted where nature was concerned.

By scraping around wildly with his legs, he found a foothold and was able to cling to the face of the slope. Then he freed his jacket and managed to get his hat back on. His breath seared his lungs and the wind knifed into him. Snow formed into slush under his gloves as he slowly began to work his way downwards. It was impossible to see above him. Once he lifted his face and snow blinded him.

He slipped several times, scraping his knees and elbows and banged the side of his head again. But, somehow, he managed to reach the bottom more or less unscathed and found himself only a few yards from the carcass of his horse. He smelled the warm blood and its hide, but the animal was dead, its neck broken and limbs shattered.

Conant had difficulty retrieving his saddlebags and rifle from beneath the fallen horse. He had to cut the cinch strap and it took a lot of tugging and heaving before he finally freed the saddle. All the physical activity made him sweat beneath his clothes and he began to shiver as it started to chill on his flesh.

On the other hand now he had his saddlebags with their precious store of food, his canteen, war bag and the scarred, but still serviceable, rifle sheath. The Winchester itself was unmarked and had oiled rags wrapped tightly about the action. He made sure he could get the rifle free of the leather in a hurry, should it be necessary, and then took stock of his situation.

He was on foot in the mountains during a snowstorm; not a good situation by any means. But Conant had survived in the past and there was no reason why he should not do so this time. First and most important, he had to find shelter. Snow was piling up in deep drifts and the storm did not seem to be abating. He would not survive in the open.

He recalled having seen an overhanging rock with jutting boulders enclosing it on either side to form a kind of cave, just before sundown. It had been across the face of the mountain, right on the timberline, just below a clump of aspen. He figured he ought to be able to locate it again, but he didn't know how far it was. Three miles? Four? Perhaps two? It was hard to estimate how far he had come in the dark on that narrow trail with snow and wind slowing his progress.

One thing was for sure, though; however far the cave was, it would not get any closer while he stood there thinking about it.

Grunting and shivering, he took up his war bag and saddlebags, and carrying his rifle, started plodding through the snowdrifts, feeling the strengthening wind and knowing that, if he did not find shelter within an hour and a half or so, he would not ever be needing it again.

Newspaperman Clive Burch was nervous. This would be the most important issue ever of the *East Valley City Dispatch*, and he knew he would make some deadly enemies once it hit the streets. Maybe he was crazy to go ahead and publish what he had learned. But the way he saw it, he had no choice now. He could not – would not – back down. Maybe he was just plain stubborn, but he had said he would expose the group who were corrupting the town and as they had made no effort to correct the situation, he had to carry out his threat.

But it was not easy to do, especially since Annie had turned up out of the blue. When he had been alone, it had not seemed to matter so much. Whatever the results of his crusading, he had only himself to think about. But now that Annie was here …

Bending over the type case with his setting stick clutched firmly in his left hand, Burch felt his belly knot up as the front door rattled. At first he figured it was only the wind, but even before the thought had fully formed, he knew he was fooling himself: the wind was coming from the other direction. There was someone out on the dark porch of the newspaper offices. He cursed himself for not having had enough sense to leave a lantern burning out there. At least it would have illuminated anyone who came onto the porch.

The door rattled again and Burch swallowed, glanced down at the old cap-and-ball Navy Colt pistol he had placed beside him. He was no good with guns. Never had been. The Colt had not been fired in years.

The door rattled again and his right hand swiftly covered the smooth cedar gun butt as he spun towards the door.

'S-someone there?' he called, voice croaking a little.

'Sure as hell is,' announced a muffled, strange voice. 'I'm freezin' out here, mister. Sorry to trouble you but yours seems to be the only place in town that's showin' a light.'

'What'd you want?' asked Burch, hefting the gun awkwardly in both hands now, tongue flicking across his dry lips. He was a balding man in his forties, his furrowed brow and eyes shadowed by a worn blue shade, ink deeply ingrained into his stubby fingers and spotting his shirt and calico apron. He tried to control the tremors that shook his lean body and knew they were not due to the cold weather: he was scared and he didn't mind admitting it to himself.

'Listen, mister, I fell off my horse outside of town,' the stranger's voice announced, and there was a catch in it now, as though he was in pain. 'Busted my shoulder, I reckon, and maybe a rib or two. I-I lost sight of my bronc in the snow. Lucky I even located the town, I guess. Can you point out the sawbones' place for me or – or somethin'? I-I'm about plumb tuckered out.'

Clive Burch crossed the room, cocking the Navy Colt awkwardly, pressing against the wall beside the front window and standing on tiptoe to see above the opaque paint, out into the stormy night. It was too dark. He could make out the head and shoulders of a man outside the door, but that was all.

'Mister?' the voice called again. 'Hell sakes … Help me, please? I don't want nothin' from you. Just directions how to find the doc.'

Burch's humane instincts got the better of him. If that man really was hurt he shouldn't be left out in the bitter cold on a night like this, suffering. Anyway, Burch told himself, he had a cocked pistol in his hands, didn't he? He could easily control the situation.

Clive Burch fumbled so badly, trying to shoot back the door bolt and juggle the pistol at the same time, that he finally lowered the hammer and rammed the Colt into his waistband, so he could use both hands. He meant to draw the gun again before he opened the door. He didn't get the chance.

Lannan's boot slammed against the door as soon as he heard the bolt withdrawn. Clive Burch grunted as he was hit by the heavy timber door and sent staggering halfway down the room, slamming his back against the printing press. Gus Lannan's six gun was in his hand as he stepped inside and kicked the door closed behind him. He fired two shots and the newspaperman was lifted up onto the rollers of the printing press by the force of the bullets. His eyes were bulging wildly as he slid slowly downwards and thudded to his knees on the floor, hands clasped to the wounds in his chest. Gus Lannan stepped across, placed the muzzle of the smoking Colt against Burch's head and dropped hammer, finishing the job.

He immediately went to the lamp and turned down the flame so that most of the big, long room was in shadow. He took the lamp across to the street-fronted cupboard he had been told to look for, smashed off the padlock and opened the doors.

He saw the cash box, but didn't pick it up. He rummaged swiftly amongst the piles of papers, looking for the brass-bound Morocco-covered book.

Then he heard a noise from the narrow door at the far end of the building. He spun towards the door, whipping up his Colt and cursing because he hadn't taken time to replace three spent cartridges. He saw a sleepy-eyed girl pulling a wrap about her slim body as she blinked in the light of the lantern she held.

'Pa?' she called. 'You all right...?' Then she saw Lannan and opened her mouth to scream.

Gus Lannan brought up his gun, at the same time sweeping the lamp from the top of the cabinet. It shattered and burst into flames. He jumped back and his shot was wild, the bullet chewing splinters from the edge of the door frame beside the girl. She almost fell back through the doorway, but had enough presence of mind to slam the door behind her. Lannan swore as flames spread through the print shop, licking at the oil-soaked floorboards.

He didn't even bother with the cash box as he heard the girl screaming beyond the door. The hell with it, he thought. He had killed that old newspaperman and that was what he was being paid for. Let that crooked sheriff handle everything else that had gone wrong.

He was getting out of here and fast.

Lannan leapt over the body of Burch and wrenched open the door. He plunged out into the street, hearing the flames gathering strength behind him, crackling as they took hold. He swiftly got his bearings as he ran along the boardwalk, seeing that a few folk were making an appearance, likely having been awakened by the successive shots. Gus Lannan swore again, skidded to a halt as he passed the alley mouth he wanted, spun, stumbled into the alley and pounded down towards the end, where the sheriff should be waiting for him.

He saw the horse and breathed a sigh of relief. At least he would make a clean getaway.

Then a gun blasted out of the darkness of the alley and he knew they had double-crossed him. They had no intention of letting him get of town alive.

The sheriff had probably seen the flames in the newspaper office and heard the last shot Lannan had taken at the girl, and realized something had gone wrong. So he figured to get himself a scapegoat.

The killer threw himself flat as the gun blasted two

more times; he heard the bullets whiz by his ears and thud into the clapboards. He rolled onto his belly and cut loose with his last two rounds at the gun flashes. He saw the sheriff duck back out of sight and came up to his knees. Swiftly he reloaded his pistol, then jumped up and ran on down the alley. Like all killers, he felt able to cope with anything the lawman had in mind, now that he had a loaded gun in his fist again.

The sheriff was coming after him. Lannan could hear his running footsteps. He turned his head and caught a glimpse of the lawman through a break in the swirling snow. He took a snap shot; saw the sheriff stumble and then he was leaping for the reins of the tethered horse. He wasn't really surprised to find it wasn't a fresh mount, but his own weary horse that he had ridden to town earlier. So it seemed his first idea was wrong. The sheriff hadn't double-crossed him on the spur of the moment; this had all the marks of pre-planning.

Lannan hit leather hard, wrenched the animal's head around hearing shouting back on Main Street and seeing the flickering light of flames as the newspaper office burned. Swearing, he turned back down the alley and his gun sought out the sheriff who was just clearing a fence and dropping into a yard beyond. Lannan snapped two shots at him and thundered away into the night.

The sheriff kicked out a paling in the fence and emptied his gun after the fleeing killer, then ran back across the yard towards Main Street, where now there was a lot of yelling as a bucket brigade was formed in front of the blazing newspaper offices.

It was not until he had cleared town and was nearing the timbered slopes of the hills that Gus Lannan realized one of the crooked lawman's last shots had hit the horse burning a deep, bloody groove across its rump.

Blood splashed down the animal's legs and left easy-to-follow crimson blotches against the white snow. If the sheriff gathered a posse, Lannan knew he was in bad trouble.

Real bad. And the lawman would make sure he wasn't taken alive.

CHAPTER 4

The bucket brigade managed to control the fire and confine it to the printing shop section of the newspaper offices, although part of the editorial offices and the living quarters upstairs were damaged.

'What in the hell happened, Sheriff?' asked a sweating man who had been in the van of the bucket brigade. 'I ain't had time to stop long enough to spit. Heard you doin' some shootin' …'

'Some ranny up to no damn good in the newspaper office. Shot down Clive Burch, and then I guess he got disturbed when he was looking for money. Clive's daughter, Annie, apparently had arrived from Blall City just after dark. Guess the killer thought Clive was alone. She disturbed him, it seems. I ain't had much of a chance to question her yet. She's with Doc Staab and some of the women. Shook her up some. The killer shot at her a few times too.'

'Judas Priest!' breathed the townsman. 'Shootin' at a woman!' He paused to nod as a man in a long fur coat and cap came up. 'Evening, Alonzo.'

Alonzo Conway, the saloon keeper, ignored the man,

looking straight into the lawman's eye. 'Heap of trouble, Sheriff,' he allowed.

'Not too much,' the lawman said, walking away, the saloon man following closely.

When they were out of earshot of the other townsmen who were checking over the still smoldering newspaper offices, the saloon keeper grabbed the sheriff's arm tightly.

'What the hell happened, Ocie? There wasn't supposed to be a goddamn fire or all that shooting.'

Sheriff Ocie Kramer pulled his arm free irritably. 'That damn Burch girl. No one told me she arrived on the Blall City stage. She walked in on Lannan, I guess, before he had a chance to get his hands on anything. I have been trying to get to the cabinet to look for the book, but there're too many fellers stompin' around in there, makin' sure there's no more small fires still burnin'.'

Alonzo Conway cursed. 'You ain't got the durn book then!'

'No.'

'Hell's bells! Darrow won't be happy to hear that, for sure. And what was all that shooting down the alley about? You get Lannan?'

The sheriff's lips pulled back from his yellow teeth as he shook his head briefly. 'Son of a bitch was too damn fast for me. And I mean fast! He almost nailed me. Had to dive for cover and, by then, he was on his mount and hightailin' it.'

'For Christ's sakes get after him then,' Conway commanded.

'He won't get too far. I hit his horse, that I am sure of,' Kramer replied.

'The hell with his horse! We want Lannan dead, so he can't relate what he knows.'

'Aw, he'll keep on ridin', I reckon. He won't stop this side of Cheyenne,' Kramer added.

Alonzo Conway poked his forefinger hard into the sheriff's chest, making him stagger. 'You want to bet your life on that? 'Cause that's what you're doin', Ocie. Lannan's a mean one and he ain't gonna take kindly to you tryin' to double-cross him. You give him all the money?'

'Nah, nah. I played it like we said, gave him half and told him I would pay the other half on his way out a' town. Left his horse tied up at the end of the alley to entice him down, but he was comin' too fast and he spotted me.'

'You blamed fool!' Conway hissed. 'You've put us all in danger now. Get after him and finish him off.'

'In this!' Kramer gestured to the snow swirling about them.

'In a goddamn hurricane if necessary!' Conway snarled. 'Make sure you shut Lannan's mouth for good. Look out, here's that deputy of yours.'

A tall young man came panting up the street, waving at the lawman and saloon keeper. He was Cooper McCarty, Kramer's deputy, an enthusiastic young man who hoped one day to wear a sheriff's star of his own.

'Sheriff,' he panted as he skidded to a halt. 'I seen you had things mostly under control here, so I been over to Doc Staab's to see Annie Burch. She's calmed down some now. She got a look at the hombre who killed her father.'

Kramer and Conway exchanged a swift glance. The sheriff tried to sound enthusiastic. 'Good, Cooper. She describe him to you?'

'As well as she could. Tall hombre in a fur-lined, canvas jacket with a stained hat, she thinks was sort of grey. She only caught a glimpse of his face, but she says he had stubble and had a kind of wolfish, hatchet-blade face ...'

Kramer waited as the deputy paused. He frowned. 'And...?'

Cooper McCarty shrugged. 'That's it. All she had time to see. He took a shot at her then and she slammed the door. You ask me, Annie done mighty good considering ...'

'Yeah,' Kramer said slowly, winking slightly at the saloon keeper. 'Yeah, I guess she did at that. Not much to go on, though. Must be a hundred men that would fit that description.'

'True, but not in this town,' McCarty said. 'I reckon we ought to get a posse together and try to run the varmint down, Sheriff. He can't get too far in this storm and it'll be blowin' a lot harder out there.'

'That's a sound idea, Sheriff,' Alonzo Conway said soberly. 'He won't be expecting a posse to come after him right away in this kind of weather, so he might not run his horse too fast. And if, as you think, you winged the animal ...'

'You hit the horse, Sheriff?' McCarty broke in. 'Hell, we gotta get after him right away then! We will have him on the run to ground before sun up. I'll start callin' for volunteers right away.'

'You do that, Cooper,' Kramer said and the eager deputy ran off towards the tight knot of townsmen still gathered outside the partially burned newspaper offices.

'Bring him back dead, Ocie,' Conway muttered to the

sheriff, as he prepared to move away. 'Then you can keep the second half of that money you didn't pay Lannan.'

Kramer's eyes narrowed. 'I figure it ought to be mine anyway.'

'Only if you bring Lannan back dead,' Conway said flatly. 'Adios, Sheriff. I'll look forward to your report come morning.'

'Don't take that uppity attitude with me, Alonzo! We're all in this together!'

Conway looked briefly over his shoulder at the lawman. 'You see this trouble is all cleared up pronto, Ocie. Or you'll find out just how uppity I can be. And you'll have Darrow and Isaac Powell to contend with, as well.'

Ocie Kramer swore under his breath as the fur-clad saloon keeper moved away down the dark, wind-whipped street. The trouble was he knew Conway wasn't bluffing. If he didn't tie up the loose ends with Lannan now, he would be a dead man within twenty-four hours.

Gus Lannan knew the horse wasn't going to make it over the mountains and he could not make a run for the pass because he figured they would be watching it. He swore again as he felt the blood on the horse's flank. The wound wasn't serious, but it was bleeding considerably, despite the bitter cold weather. With rest, the wound would heal but he could not afford to let the horse rest. However, it was obvious he couldn't run the animal until it dropped, either.

The storm seemed to be getting worse and he did not want to be riding a wounded horse on the high trails in the darkness, with a blizzard blowing. Whether he liked it or not, he would have to find somewhere to hole up for the night. Lannan swore once more as he made the decision. It was dangerous, but likely the least dangerous of the choices he had.

If he pushed on, the horse would fold up under him soon enough, he was sure of that. Or, maybe, it would step right off a cliff and they would both plunge to their deaths. Either way, he would be finished.

But, if he found someplace where he could sit out the blizzard and allow the horse to rest up, he might be able to get away. He didn't figure a posse would come after him in this storm; anyway, Kramer would probably stall them, hoping Lannan would hightail it clear out of the country. His mouth tightened when he thought about the double-cross the sheriff had tried to pull – no, had pulled – for Lannan only had half the money he had been promised, even though he had carried out his part of the bargain. He had killed the newspaperman and likely would have found that mysterious book they wanted, too, if the girl hadn't walked in on him.

It would go against the grain to just vamoose without collecting the remainder of the money. Gus Lannan figured the crooked sheriff would get out Wanted notices on him mighty fast, and generally make life hell for him in this neck of the woods. So, for now, he would have to get as far away as possible. But he would be back. He would come back and get square with that lousy sheriff for the double-cross.

Gus Lannan reined in the slow-moving horse abruptly, his right hand sweeping back the flap of his jacket, and closing about the butt of the Colt. He had seen something up ahead, through a break in the swirling snow.

'By hell! It's a campfire!' he said out loud, the words whipped away instantly by the icy wind.

He could see the warm, beckoning glow of the fire reflected from the walls of a snug rocky overhang. And there was a lone man hunkered over the fire, stirring something in a skillet. Lannan sniffed and his mouth filled with saliva as he caught the savoury odour of frying beans and the aromatic aroma of coffee bubbling in the blackened pot at the edge of the fire.

It was too much for Lannan. If he had been undecided before, his mind was now made up. He was not only going to rest up his bronc for the night, but he was going to sleep snug and warm and with a full belly. He could not see the man's horse, but it would be tethered someplace nearby. Come morning, he would decide whether he rode away with two horses, keeping his own wounded mount for a spare, or just helped himself to the stranger's fresh mount and abandoned his own.

That food really got to Lannan. It had been hours since he had eaten and he was plum tired to boot, cold and savagely angry about the double-cross pulled on him. This loner was just what he needed: someone on whom to vent his frustrated anger, as well as supplying him with vittles and a fresh mount. What more could he have asked for? He dismounted and slid his Colt from its holster. He kept hold of the wounded horse's reins, afraid to release it in case it wandered off in the snowstorm and he couldn't find it again. For Lannan, for all his confidence, was a cautious man and he knew nothing was ever quite as it seemed. He didn't aim for this loner to get the upper hand, but, just in case it happened, he wanted to have his own horse, wounded though it was, within reach.

Warily, he stalked forward, floundering knee-deep across the snowbound slope, closing in on the warm, ruddy glow beneath the overhang of rock where the campfire burned.

Reason Conant stirred the beans in the skillet once more and saw they were beginning to blacken. It was time to start eating, but he had wanted to make sure they were well heated before he did so. The coffee was bubbling and he moved the pot slightly away from the fire, then picked up another sapling and threw it on the flames.

The fire flared and he moved back as the resin boiled out of the wood, spitting and igniting. This overhang had been a mighty good choice and he was glad he had been able to find it again after the long, freezing trek back from the high trail where he had lost his mount. Not only had he located the shelter, he had also found stacks of saplings and small branches against the rear wall, obviously having been left there by some other lonely traveller at an earlier time.

He had his grub sack and now a good warm fire, the heat reflecting back from the rocks, and he knew he would sleep snug this night. Even if the snow banked up at the entrance, he would be warm and tomorrow, if the weather eased, he would try to make his way to the pass on foot. If the blizzard was still blowing, he would stay put. He would sit it out. He had enough food for a few days if he rationed it carefully.

He forked up some of the beans and was munching on his second mouthful when he became aware of the figure materializing out of the darkness outside. He froze when he saw the gun in the man's hand, the firelight glinting from the barrel. There was a horse behind the man and the animal looked weak and exhausted.

That was all Reason had a chance to see. Gus Lannan jerked the Colt barrel.

'Just set the skillet down easy-like feller, then move back gentle.'

Reason knew right away he had trouble. This wasn't just some drifter like himself, caught out in the storm. This man was too wary for that. He wasn't going to take any chances on Reason tossing the skillet of beans or the coffee pot in his direction. He saw the man's eyes flickering around the cave, taking in the war bag and rifle still in its scabbard leaning against the rock and dirt wall. The gun jerked impatiently.

'Set down that there skillet, goddamn you!' Lannan snapped.

Reason did so and eased his hands gently away from the handle. Then, still on his haunches, worked his way back a few paces.

'Better,' Lannan said. He tightened his grip on the Colt and Reason Conant braced himself for the shot, but the man hesitated. 'Where's your horse?'

'Don't have one,' the drifter replied simply.

Lannan's face showed anger. 'Don't get smart with me, mister!'

'He walked off a high trail a couple of hours ago,' Reason explained. 'I remembered passin' this cave and made my way back here. Look, if you just want some grub and to get warm, come on in. No need for the gun ...'

'The hell there ain't!' snapped Gus Lannan, studying Reason's hawk-like face carefully. 'Goddamn, you're talkin' gospel, ain't you?'

Reason Conant shrugged.

Lannan's mouth tightened up. 'Well, it just makes it much easier, you side-winder!'

He raised the Colt slowly, deliberately, aiming at Reason. The drifter knew he was a breath away from death, but he was damned if he was going to just stand there and let this son of a gun kill him.

Abruptly, he let out a blood-curdling, high-pitched yell and the sound was magnified many times by the confining walls of the cave. It caught Lannan off-guard and scared the hell out of him. As well, the wounded horse reared and whinnied and the jerking on the reins pulled Lannan off-balance. His Colt exploded and the bullet drove into the earthen roof of the cave. Reason, at that instant he let loose the war whoop, flung himself backwards thanking his lucky stars now for the missing rawhide ties on his jacket front. It made it much easier for his hand to drag the flap back hard enough to break the lower tie, giving him full access to his holstered Colt.

Gus Lannan had his smoking Colt cocked for a second shot now, but Reason's Colt blasted and the killer jerked as lead burned across his ribs. His gun exploded into the floor of the cave, scattering part of the fire and making the coffee pot jump. Reason rolled back to the rear wall then brought the Colt across his body and chopped at the hammer spur with the edge of his left hand.

In that confined space and at such short range, the Colt sent four fast shots smashing into Lannan. He jerked and spun as the lead struck home, the last bullet taking him through the middle of the face. His head jerked back and his body was flung clear off the ledge at the cave entrance and into the darkness. The horse was whinnying and prancing as Reason came to his feet, smoking gun in his hand. There was only one shot remaining. But he knew he wouldn't be needing it.

He stood on the ledge and looked out into the lashing snow, instinctively pulling his jacket across his chest as the bitter wind knifed into him. Gus Lannan was spread eagled in the snow below and already snowflakes were settling on the body. Reason turned towards the horse that had begun to nuzzle him. Holstering his Colt, he picked up the animal's reins.

'Come on in, big feller. I dunno who your master was, but he sure was none too friendly. Let's get you in here out of the cold and – hell almighty!' Reason broke off and whistled softly when he saw the caked blood on the horse's rump. He gently touched the groove in the flesh. 'I'd say a bullet did that ...' He glanced briefly down the slope at the dim shape of the dead man. 'Looks like your master might have been on the run ... Well, he's stopped runnin' now and you, old friend, have found yourself shelter for the night. Come on in, while I build up the fire.'

CHAPTER 5

The blizzard blew all night and had scarcely diminished in intensity by the time a dimly seen and watery sun shed its pale light across the high country.

Reason Conant had slept warm and snug and the horse had found a corner of the cave where it had spent the night. The fire had burned down, but Reason built it up and set the coffee pot on the flames. Then he went outside and, ignoring the snow that spat all around him, looked down the slope where Gus Lannan had fallen after the shoot-out last night.

There was no sign of the outlaw's body. It had been buried deep under the snow.

He shrugged as he returned to the cave. That problem was solved anyway. He had no regrets about the man he had killed. It had been self-defence and, while he was curious about why the stranger had wanted to kill him, he wasn't going to let it bother him. After breakfast, he searched through Lannan's saddlebags and found them empty of grub. But, in the bottom of one, he located the oilskin package of money and whistled softly when he saw how much it amounted to.

Now, he started to worry. There was over two hundred dollars in the package, which was a hell of a lot more than a saddle tramp like the stranger should be carrying. Then there was the wound on the horse ... Reason figured maybe the man had robbed a bank or something and had been on the run, which would explain his jumpiness and willingness to kill – and also his interest in Reason's horse. With a wounded mount, he would be looking for a fresh one.

Reason pursed his lips, stuffed the money back inside the oilskin and then, after some hesitation, put the package in his own saddlebag. He took Lannan's bags from the saddle and flung them into a corner. He shook the man's heavy canteen, expecting to hear the slosh of liquid, but instead there was only a dry rasping around. Curious, Reason uncapped the metal bottle and tilted it slightly.

Dry sand trickled out from the canteen.

He was more puzzled than ever. No grub in the saddlebags and a canteen full of sand ... it began to look as if someone hadn't wanted the man to survive in the hills.

Reason flung the canteen into the corner near the empty saddlebags and saddled the horse, using some of the water from his own canteen to wash the animal's wound. He could see the raw furrow in the hide clearly now and although the bleeding had stopped, the horse appeared to be having trouble moving its rear legs.

But Reason Conant wanted to get moving along the trail. He felt uneasy here now. There was something strange about the man he had to shoot and he figured he would rather brave the blizzard than stay where he was and maybe have some of the man's friends – or his enemies – turn up.

Of course, once he led the horse into the snow, Reason began to have doubts about the wisdom of his decision. It was bitterly cold, the wind moaned eerily through the timber and canyons and the snow swirled thickly, blotting out the trail. He mounted gingerly. The horse protested, but settled down when he caressed its neck and spoke quietly in its ear. Then he urged the animal slowly down the slope, glancing once towards the deep snowdrift that covered Lannan's body.

He sure hoped that the stranger wasn't going to bring him a load of grief.

His idea this time was to go through the pass instead of trying to cross the mountain. He wanted to get to Biggs as quickly as possible, where he aimed to hide the wounded horse outside of town, then slip in on foot and see if he could find out what was going on. He had a feeling that if he arrived in town on a wounded horse, with all that money on him, he might be in for trouble.

The money began to bother him more and more as the horse plodded along the trail, picking its way through the snow that still fell in blinding white sheets.

The wind dropped as he rode into the lee of the mountains and through a break in the snow, he was able to see the pass up ahead. The trees stood out starkly against the white landscape and most of the rocks were buried under drifts of snow. It might be tough going, even through the pass. And Biggs lay only ten miles beyond across fairly flat country, according to information he had been given.

Reason kneed the limping mount towards a pile of snow-dusted boulders, gloved fingers fumbling awkwardly

43

at the flap of the saddlebag. He had decided to stash the money – at least until he had time to find out something about the stranger he had shot. He realized that the people in Biggs might know nothing about the man, but it was a good starting place. What he found out would determine what he did with the money.

Reason had been playing his hunches for a long time and he had a strong one now that unless he was mighty careful, he could find himself in a heap of trouble.

He was right, of course. And it came a lot sooner than he anticipated.

Reason Conant dismounted by the boulders, searching for a good place to hide the money. He waded through knee-deep snow and was reaching out for a particularly buried rock to steady himself when something erupted inches from his gloved fingers. The drifter snatched his hand back instinctively, as grit stung his face and, at the same instant, he heard the muffled whip crack of a rifle. He spun so fast that he stumbled against the rock. The rifle cracked again and he felt his hat brim jerk as lead pierced the felt.

He saw the horseman then, on a ledge up-slope, towards the pass. The shooting had brought others out from behind trees and rocks on the slope, where they had probably been searching. A half dozen guns hammered just as the wind began to howl again and swirls of snow whipped in between the drifter and the shooters.

Reason Conant didn't hesitate. He dropped the money and floundered back towards his horse, knowing he had little hope of outdistancing the hostile riders, whoever they were. But if the snow kept coming in such blinding sheets, he might manage to find someplace to hide.

He heard shouts and the guns began firing again as he clambered into the saddle. The horse was nervous, sensing his alarm, but he spoke soothingly, crouched over the animal's neck and slammed his heels into its flanks. The horse made a valiant effort to leap forward, but its rear legs weren't working properly and it floundered, so that Reason had to literally haul it upright by the reins before it broke into a run.

Cursing, he glanced over his shoulder and saw a band of men charging down the slope as the snow eased. Guns hammered and he heard the zip of several bullets burying themselves in the snow about his racing horse's feet. He palmed up his six gun, hipped in the saddle and loosed off two shots. They were answered by a volley that sent lead whipping past his face. Then he was into the timber and a large chunk of bark flew from an elm on his left, leaving a jagged white scar on the trunk. Other bullets shook the snow-laden branches above him.

Reason tried to weave the mount through the timber, but the animal was incapable of the manoeuvre and he knew that if he didn't find somewhere to hole up quickly, he was going to be in bad trouble.

The horse was slowing. Its legs were sliding this way and that as it tried to increase its pace to satisfy Reason's constant urging. But the wound had weakened it too much and Reason knew it wasn't going to outrun his pursuers.

There was a sudden flurry to his right and, at first, he thought it was a heavy swirl of snow. Too late, he glimpsed the horseman who leapt his mount from the trees and, with a yell, rammed into Reason's horse. The wounded horse whinnied and began to fall. Reason had no chance.

As the horse went down, he went with it, instinctively kicking his boots free of the stirrups and flinging himself away from the falling body.

Wet snow crunched against his face and he spat out a mouthful, as he tried to get to his feet. The man who rammed Reason's mount rode forward and kicked him behind the ear, sending the drifter sprawling once more. He rolled onto his back, bringing up his Colt instinctively, but freezing as he looked down the barrel of a cocked Winchester.

The man behind the rifle loomed large and bulky, and his voice was cold as he grated, 'One more move, you son of a bitch, and I'll blow your head clear off your shoulders.'

Reason froze and opened his gloved fingers, allowing his Colt to fall into the snow. The rifle barrel jerked and he clambered slowly to his feet. As he did so, he saw the brass star on the rider's jacket front. Breath hissed through his nostrils as he kept his hands at shoulder level.

'Take it easy, Sheriff. I ain't done nothing,' he rasped.

'Not much, you ain't!' snapped his captor, lifting his head at the sound of approaching riders. 'Over here, Sheriff!' he called and lowered the rifle a little as the horsemen made their way through the trees.

'Shoot the dog!' shouted someone as he approached.

'Yeah, Cooper, put a bullet in him. We'll look the other way and say he was tryin' to escape or kill you.'

Reason felt the blood drain from his face as he looked into Cooper McCarty's taut features.

'Hey, hold up, damn it! You got the wrong man,' Reason protested.

'The hell we have,' growled the young deputy, his

eyes searching the posse men for Sheriff Ocie Kramer. He gestured to the horse Reason had been riding. 'That horse has a bullet burn across the rump. And you're a tall hombre in a canvas jacket, with beard stubble and a narrow face. You fit the description of the man we want, mister ...'

'No, wait, I can explain ...' Reason began but then the sheriff came riding into the group, holding the dripping oilskin package of money.

The lawman drew rein abruptly and his face showed genuine shock when he saw Reason Conant: he had been expecting to confront Gus Lannan. He switched his gaze swiftly towards McCarty.

'We got him, all right, Sheriff!' McCarty said, obviously very pleased with himself. 'He didn't see me in the trees and I rode the varmint down. What's that you got there?'

'Huh? Oh, this is what he was tryin' to stash in the rocks back there. Money,' the sheriff said.

'Lot of money looks like too,' opined a shivering member of the posse. 'Let's get back to town where it's warm and sort it out there, huh?'

The sheriff's gaze bored into Reason Conant's face. 'Who are you, feller?'

'Reason Conant, Sheriff. I ...' he began to reply.

'What're you doin' in these hills?' Kramer asked.

'Tryin' to find my way to Biggs.'

Sheriff Kramer gestured to the wounded horse, whose reins were now being held by a posse man. 'That's your horse?'

'No, but I was riding it,' Reason explained.

'How'd it get that wound on its rump?' Kramer asked

47

harshly, mentally cursing the deputy for capturing this drifter alive – whoever he was. The sheriff didn't know what in hell had happened to Lannan, but he knew this was the killer's horse. And he would rather have had Reason shot down in cold blood, so that he couldn't say anything. The posse men would have been satisfied, figuring they had avenged Clive Burch's murder. But now, thanks to that fool Cooper McCarty's eagerness for glory, this drifter was alive and going to spill some story that could only complicate matters. Ocie Kramer's brain raced as he tried to think of a way out of this mess.

'I dunno how the horse was wounded,' Reason admitted. 'Listen, I lost my own mount off a high trail last night and I managed to get to a cave ...'

'We don't want any of your lies, you lousy scum!' cut in McCarty harshly and, for once, Kramer approved of his young deputy. McCarty brutally rammed the barrel of his rifle into Reason's midriff, causing the drifter to gasp and double-up. 'You ain't gonna talk your way out of this!'

'String him up!' a man called from the back row of riders. 'Clive Burch was a good friend to all of us!'

'Yeah, Sheriff,' said another man, 'how's about you and Cooper mosey along into the hills for a spell? It'll all be over when you come back. You can easy say you just couldn't get back in time to prevent the lynching. No one's gonna make any fuss about a necktie party for this murdering sidewinder.'

Other posse men shouted agreement. They were cold and weary and wanted swift vengeance for Clive Burch's cold-blooded killing.

It was obvious that Kramer was tempted and Cooper

McCarty frowned, looking swiftly at the sheriff.

'Hell, Sheriff, you can't listen to 'em! You can't consider allowing a lynch party!'

Sheriff Kramer's lips tightened. No, McCarty was right, goddamn it. He couldn't condone a lynching. Not now. Not with a go-by-the-book eager beaver deputy like Cooper McCarty present. The man wanted the glory that would go with the capture of this drifter whom Kramer aimed to charge with Burch's murder, anyway. Least ways, until he found out what had happened to Lannan.

'Listen, do I get a chance to tell my story?' shouted Reason Conant suddenly, a note of desperation in his voice. He was in more trouble than he had anticipated. 'I took that horse off ...'

Ocie Kramer spurred his mount forward suddenly and rammed the animal brutally into Reason, knocking him sprawling. The posse men cheered approval. Reason floundered in the snow and started to get to his feet.

The sheriff leaned from the saddle and smashed his gun barrel across the drifter's head. Reason dropped again, unconscious this time. Kramer looked into the puzzled face of Cooper McCarty.

'Tie him to his horse and let's get back to town. We'll settle things there.'

The deputy was pleased enough, but some of the posse men looked disappointed that there wouldn't be a hanging. Kramer made a mental note of which ones had pressed for a lynching.

If he had his way, they would not be disappointed for long.

CHAPTER 6

Reason Conant was cold. His well-muscled body shivered under the thin blanket that was draped across him on the hard narrow bunk in the Biggs jail. His head throbbed and there was a duck-egged sized lump above his left temple. He touched it gingerly and winced, sitting up carefully and pulling the blanket about his shoulders.

His teeth chattered and he realized they had stripped him of his sheepskin-lined canvas jacket and his gun belt. He staggered to the bars and shook the locked door.

'Hey!' he bawled and winced as pain knifed through his head. But he yelled again and kept on yelling until the door at the end of the passage opened and a man he recognized as the deputy entered.

'Shut up that racket,' Cooper McCarty growled. 'So you decided to join us again.'

'How about my jacket? I'm freezing,' Reason called.

'It is evidence,' the deputy fired back.

'Evidence? For what? Listen, tell me later. Just get me somethin' warm, huh? Come on, mister. I'm likely to catch my death in here.'

'Won't make no never mind if you do, not where you're

headed,' McCarty said. 'But I'll get you somethin'.'

Reason waited, pacing the confines of the cell, teeth clenched, muscles aching, head pounding. McCarty returned with three blankets and stuffed them through the bars. The drifter gratefully snatched them up and wrapped them around himself, then sat huddled on the edge of the bunk. He looked into the deputy's sober face.

'What kind of trouble am I in? I get the notion I'm supposed to have killed someone. Right?' Reason inquired.

'Look, don't waste your breath lyin' to me, Reason Conant. You gunned down Clive Burch and likely would've gotten away with his cash box if his daughter hadn't disturbed you. Sheriff nearly got you as you made your getaway, but only winged your horse. You been caught and identified as the killer, so just shut down and don't make any more trouble,' McCarty snapped.

Reason lunged for the bars as McCarty turned away towards the door leading to the front office. 'What the hell do you mean "identified"? I've never been to this town before.'

McCarty rounded swiftly, shaking his stiffened forefinger in Reason's direction. 'I warned you to shut down! Now you do it, mister, or it'll be worse for you. That's all I gotta say. Except, after what I seen you done to Annie Burch I-I wish I'd gone along with the posse when they wanted to lynch you!'

The deputy turned towards the front door again, but stopped and backed up into the passage. Reason, struggling with his blankets at the bars, paused and frowned as two people entered the cellblock. They were Sheriff Ocie Kramer and a flaxen-haired, hazel-eyed girl dressed in black. He guessed she was Annie Burch, the dead editor's daughter. She looked at him coolly now, her face somewhat pale and set into stiff lines. He figured her to be in her early twenties.

Kramer stepped forward and thrust Reason's sheepskin-lined canvas jacket through the bars. 'Put it on, you.'

The drifter glanced at him, then moved his gaze to the girl. He let the blankets slip from his shoulders and shrugged gratefully into his warm jacket. He saw a small crease form between her eyes.

'Put on your hat,' growled Ocie Kramer and Reason Conant turned to the bunk where his hat, with its bullet-punctured brim, lay. He jammed it on his head and looked, puzzled, through the bars at the lawman and the girl. The deputy hovered about in the background.

'Now what, Sheriff?' Reason questioned.

Kramer ignored him and turned to the girl. 'That the man, Annie?'

'I-I'm not sure, Sheriff Kramer,' she said in a quiet smooth voice. 'He-he was sort of half-turned away, with the light only just touching his face …'

'You heard Miss Burch,' McCarty snapped. 'Turn half away, drifter.'

Reason did so and at the girl's instructions, tucked his chin down towards his shoulder. He heard her step back but, as he went to turn, the sheriff snapped at him to stay where he was.

'Well?' Sheriff Kramer sounded impatient.

Reason heard the girl sigh. 'I-I'm not sure, Sheriff. He certainly looks like the man I saw rummaging through Pa's cabinet. He's about the same height, the jacket's similar and he's unshaven, but there's just something …

Maybe the hat. It might be a little darker than the one I saw.'

'Be hard to tell its colour if there wasn't enough light to see his face clearly, Annie, wouldn't it?' the lawman suggested.

'Ye-es, I suppose so,' she admitted slowly.

'It's gotta be him,' growled Kramer impatiently. 'He's just as you described and he was riding the horse I winged when he was getting away. He's our man, all right!'

'I'm not, Sheriff,' Reason said quietly, turning and looking directly into the girl's face now. 'Ma'am, I'm not the feller who killed your father. That's gospel. I've been trying to tell these men what really happened, but they won't gimme a chance …'

'You'll have your chance in court!' snapped McCarty.

'You deserve as much chance as you gave Clive Burch,' growled Kramer, his eyes very dangerous. 'Which was none at all. So just shut up and think yourself lucky a rope ain't already stretching your neck.' He turned and took Annie Burch's arm. 'C'mon, Annie.'

'No, wait.' The girl gazed steadily into Reason Conant's face, seeing the plea in his eyes. She felt somehow disturbed by his expression and a greater doubt rose within her. 'I-I'd like to hear what this man has to say.'

'Lies! He'll just tell you a pack of lies, Annie,' said Kramer. 'They'll only upset you all over again and …'

'The man who killed your father is dead!' Reason said swiftly, addressing himself to the girl and, as he had hoped, catching her full attention now. And McCarty's and Kramer's too, for that matter.

'You killed Clive Burch!' snapped Ocie Kramer.

Reason continued to address himself to the girl. 'My name's Reason Conant, ma'am. I'm a drifter, I guess. I was riding over the range last night when I got caught in that blizzard and my horse stepped off a high trail, taking me with it …'

Kramer snorted. 'There's a lie for a start! You'd be dead if you went over on your horse!'

Reason showed them the rip in his jacket. 'This snagged on a bush and I hung there until I could climb down.'

'Hogwash!' scoffed Cooper McCarty, but the girl placed a hand on the young deputy's arm, causing him to flush deeply.

'Please, Coop. Let him continue,' Annie said quietly.

'Thanks, ma'am. I got my saddlebags and rifle and made my way to a cave I had seen before sundown. Later, around ten o'clock, maybe ten-thirty, this feller appeared in the cave entrance, on foot, but holdin' the reins of that horse I was riding with the bullet burn on its rump. He put a gun on me, wanted to know where my mount was, then said he was gonna kill me for my food. I let out a war whoop to kind of startle him and shot him. The bullet knocked him clean off the ledge and by morning he was buried deep under a snowdrift. I was riding through the pass towards town when the posse jumped me. That's the truth, ma'am.'

'You were trying to stash that money when we caught up with you!' snapped Cooper McCarty.

Reason nodded. 'I'd found it in the saddlebags, which I left in that cave, by the way, if you want to check my story. And the feller's canteen was filled with sand, too.'

'Sand?' echoed McCarty, but Kramer's eyes narrowed. He said nothing. The girl seemed more bewildered than ever.

'Yeah,' continued Reason. 'It seemed to me that someone had left him high through wild country. Looked to me like he was meant to die out there in them hills, and in this weather, it wouldn't take long. And there was the wound on the horse – someone had already taken a shot at him. When I saw all that money I thought maybe he had robbed a bank. I aimed to stash it, leave the horse outside of town, then mosey in on foot and see what I could find out. I didn't want to be caught riding an out-law's horse, but that's exactly what happened. You gotta believe me, ma'am. I didn't know your father and I'd have no reason to kill him ...' He stopped suddenly, frowning intently at the girl, then continued, 'Ma'am, maybe that man was paid to kill your father. Maybe that was what the money was for. And whoever hired him figured to try to cover their own tracks by sending him into the wilderness country with no water or food.'

'That's a load of hogwash, if I ever heard one,' said Sheriff Ocie Kramer, his face hard and deadly, but inwardly marvelling that Reason had come so close to the truth.

Reason Conant ignored him and spoke to the girl. 'Was there some reason someone might want your pa dead, ma'am?'

Annie shook her head slowly. 'Not that I know of. But I've just arrived in town. I've been teaching school in another part of the state and as it was – would've been – Pa's forty-fifth birthday this week, I-I thought I would surprise him with a visit, but ...'

She choked off the words and dabbed at her suddenly moist eyes with a wispy lace handkerchief. Cooper McCarty stepped up beside her protectively, glaring at Reason.

'You just shut your face, you lyin' skunk! Annie's had enough upsets without you addin' to them,' the young deputy snapped.

As he started to lead the girl away, Reason called desperately, 'Check my story! The cave is just on the timberline, to the north of where you picked me up, I think. The body will be buried too deep, but you will find the saddlebags, the canteen filled with sand and the remains of my camp in the cave. Check it out, will you please!'

His hands were gripping the bars as Cooper McCarty led Annie Burch out through the door. Ocie Kramer stepped forward and hit him across the fingers with his gun barrel. Reason whipped his hand back swiftly, cursing, clutching the throbbing hand to his chest. He glared at the cold-eyed sheriff.

'You've had all the say you are goin' to have, mister. Just tell me one thing; you really expect us to believe that wild story?' Kramer asked.

'It's true, goddamn it!' Reason shouted.

'You claim you killed Lannan?'

'Lannan? Was that the killer's name?' When Kramer didn't answer, Reason shrugged. 'I killed the man who had been riding that horse. And he was wearing a canvas jacket like mine. You know you can buy similar ones all through this high country. His hat was maybe lighter, and he was about my size, beard stubbled, too. It would be easy for that girl to mistake me for him.'

Ocie Kramer grunted and turned away without

another word, making for the door.

'Hey, what the hell happens to me now?' called Reason with impatience.

The sheriff turned, with his hand on the edge of the door. 'That depends, mister. That depends.'

And on that enigmatic note he closed the door behind him and Reason Conant heard a key turn in the lock. Tight-lipped, he went back to the bunk, lay down and piled all the blankets on top of himself.

At least he would be warm while his fate was decided.

But he didn't feel confident: he knew he hadn't convinced either the lawman or the girl he was telling the truth.

CHAPTER 7

There weren't many drinkers in the saloon when the sheriff pushed through the bat-wings. He caught the barkeep's eye and shook his head as the man held up the lawman's private bottle. Instead, he pointed towards the beaded curtains hanging in a narrow, arched doorway. The barkeep nodded and the lawman pushed the strings of the beads aside and knocked perfunctorily on the door behind them, before turning the knob and stepping into Alonzo Conway's private office.

The saloon keeper was seated behind his desk, lighting a cheroot, a shot glass of whiskey on the polished wood before him. There was another man seated opposite Conway and he, too, held a glass of whiskey, turning it slowly between this thick fingers. He was big and beefy, with particularly heavy shoulders that strained at the seams of the broadcloth, claw hammer coat he wore. His face was rugged, his hair short, curly and unruly. He was in his forties and he was as tough as he looked. His name was Gideon Darrow and he managed the Golden Cloud Mine Company in the hills outside town.

Darrow and Conway both looked expectantly at the

sheriff as the lawman made his way to the sideboard and poured himself a drink from Conway's decanter. He tossed it down in one gulp, then refilled the glass before turning towards the two hard-faced men.

'His name's Reason Conant. Claims he's a drifter. Says he killed Lannan in a gunfight last night,' Sheriff Ocie Kramer said simply.

The miner and saloon keeper straightened in their chairs.

'You believe him?' asked Darrow, his voice deep and rumbling.

Kramer hesitated. 'He looks pretty tough. But the way he told it, he would have had to outdraw Lannan. And I dunno … Lannan was mighty fast. But he described Lannan well, and his empty saddlebags and the canteen filled with sand. He also had the money that I'd paid to Lannan and he was forkin' Lannan's horse. Yeah. I reckon he was speakin' gospel.'

'Then we got no worries,' Conway said, obviously relieved. He grinned tightly around his cheroot, picked up his glass and held it aloft. 'To our success then, gents. All we gotta do now is get our hands on that book of Clive Burch's.'

Darrow looked sharply at the sheriff as Kramer hesitated to drink. 'Somethin' wrong, Ocie?' The miner's eyes were narrowed, his rugged face tense as he tried to read the sheriff's expression.

Kramer looked uncomfortable. 'I dunno as our worries are over. This Conant planted a bug in Annie Burch's ear that Lannan might have been paid to kill her father.'

'How the hell did he get that notion?' demanded Conway hotly.

Kramer raised a placating hand. 'It just seemed to hit him while he was talking, tryin' to explain the money Lannan had on him. I mean, I couldn't say Lannan had robbed a bank or a stage. I tried earlier to plant the notion in the gal's head that it'd been taken from her father's cash box. But she insisted that the box was still locked and intact and that Clive Burch had never kept cash with his mortgage payments on the newspaper building. She would never go along with the idea that it had been stolen from Clive.'

'So you just didn't try to explain it,' said Gideon Darrow tightly.

'I didn't know how,' admitted Kramer. 'I wouldn't have even picked up the damn package, except I was ridin' with one of the posse and he said we had better take a look at what Conant had been trying to hide when he was spotted. With witnesses, I couldn't just hide it.'

'You damn well could have tried!' growled Alonzo Conway.

But Gideon Darrow shook his head slowly. 'No, Ocie did right. He had to bring the money out in the open, once someone else had seen it. This Conant would have mentioned it anyway. What do you make of him, Ocie? He what he says?'

Ocie Kramer shrugged. 'Looks like a drifter. A tough feller, I'd say, and if he did outgun Lannan ...' He pursed his lips and whistled softly. 'Like I said – tough.'

'Well, if Lannan's dead,' said Conway, 'what the hell's there to worry about? He sure won't be talking and no one else can prove anything.'

'You fool!' growled Darrow and Conway seemed to cower a little under the big miner's deadly glare. 'If that girl follows up the notion that someone was hired to kill her father, she might get her hands on the book. And once she does that, she will know damn well who paid Lannan that money.' He turned his bleak gaze to the sheriff. 'We should have played it straight with him – paid him off and let him get away.'

'Aw, we talked all that out before we brought him in, Gideon,' the sheriff replied shortly. 'We agreed it was risky letting a man like Lannan roam around knowing what he did. And, anyway, we didn't have his full fee.'

Darrow stood up and began pacing the small office, big hands clasped behind his back. He stopped abruptly and looked soberly at the other two.

'We played it the way we saw it and we fouled up. We gotta face that. But Lannan's dead—'

'We hope,' put in Kramer.

'Should be easy enough to check out – on the quiet, though. I think it might be to our advantage to frame Burch's killing on this drifter, after all.'

Alonzo Conway stiffened in his chair. 'That's kind of dangerous, Gideon! If he gets a smart lawyer ...'

Darrow merely glared and the saloon keeper stopped in mid-sentence, flushing. 'The town liked Clive Burch. They will feel better if they think they helped bring his killer to "justice".' He smiled crookedly. 'You're right, Alonzo, about it being too dangerous to turn Conant loose in a courtroom with a smart lawyer, but that doesn't have to happen.'

He paused, flicking his gaze from one to the other as he let his words sink in.

'A necktie party!' breathed Conway.

'Now, wait up!' Sheriff Kramer said. 'I'm sheriff here. I

got Conant in my jail. I gotta watch out for myself. If I let a lynch mob bust him loose …'

'You don't have to be here,' Darrow pointed out.

Kramer scowled. 'I sure as hell couldn't leave Cooper McCarty in charge. He's young, but he's as ambitious as hell and he wouldn't let any lynch mob near the jailhouse.'

'Find him somethin' to do out of town, damn it,' growled Darrow impatiently. 'Send him out to look for that cave and check if Lannan's body's there.'

'It's buried under several feet of snow, according to the drifter. But I guess I could send him out there. He could look for the saddlebags and canteen Conant left in the cave. Don't much matter whether Cooper finds 'em or not. By the time he gets back, the necktie party should be all over, huh?'

'That's right.' Darrow turned to Conway. 'I'll have Isaac Powell come in with some of the rougher boys and plenty of dough. He will be primed to work them up and you can help by planting a few men amongst the town's drinkers, Alonzo. Stir them up, set up some free booze. Then stand back and let Powell do the rest.'

Conway nodded slowly, obviously not too pleased with his role. 'All right. I guess if anyone can pull it off, it'll be Powell.'

'What about me?' asked Kramer, a little anxious. 'I can't be in town, but I've got to have a damn good excuse for not being here!'

Darrow waved it aside. 'I will arrange for some trouble at the mine that needs your attention urgently. You will be investigating that while the trouble's on in town.'

'A County Sheriff or US Marshal will investigate, you

know,' Kramer pointed out. 'They always do when there's a lynching. They'll want to know why I left a prisoner in an unguarded jail.'

'Hell almighty! Have I got to think of everything?' snarled Darrow. 'Look, you will have already sent Cooper out to the cave. Right? I will send in word you are needed urgently because of serious trouble out at the mine. You will grab some stupid townsman, deputize him, shove a Greener in his hands and tell him to guard the prisoner till you get back, because the mine trouble can't wait. That good enough for you? Heavens to Betsy!'

Kramer flushed and nodded curtly. 'It'll work, I guess.'

''Course it will work,' replied Darrow sharply.

'Listen, wouldn't it be a whole sight easier if this Conant character was just shot tryin' to escape?' suggested the saloon keeper.

'No. That would mean I'd have to do it,' said Kramer. 'McCarty wouldn't shoot to kill and I don't want to be involved in this any deeper than I already am.'

'We're all in deep,' Darrow pointed out. 'But a lynching's the best idea, Alonzo. Get the town worked up and, with Isaac Powell's prodding, they will do the job for us.'

Conway still seemed unconvinced. 'I don't see that Conant's any real danger to us.'

'Mebbe not, but it will satisfy the town – and it will make damn sure he don't become a danger to us. He sounds like the kind of feller who would poke his nose into things, just to find out what happened, if he was to be turned loose now. We can't risk that, and he's already got the girl suspicious.'

'She's gonna be a danger – 'specially if she finds that

book of Clive's,' pointed out the sheriff.

'You sure it didn't burn in the fire?' Darrow asked.

'I ain't had a chance for a good look, but I'd say we'd be just too lucky if that happened. I reckon we can't risk it. We've got to get it first.'

'Well, you are the sheriff. You got a right to sift through the ashes, looking for "evidence" … Go and do it.'

Kramer heaved a sigh. 'Me again. My neck seems to be on the block a helluva lot.'

'Yeah? What about mine?' demanded Conway. 'I ain't keen on having any part in stirring up that lynch mob.'

'All our necks are on the line,' growled Darrow. 'That's why we had to silence Burch in the first place. Now quit griping and let's get this thing rolling. If you can't find the book, Ocie, maybe the girl will have an accident, too, just to tie up loose ends.'

Conway shook his head slowly. He felt it was getting out of hand.

'I kinda of like the girl,' Kramer announced.

Darrow gave him a bleak look. 'Then you take care of her,' he said in a deadly tone.

Ocie Kramer dropped his gaze uneasily.

CHAPTER 8

Everything smelled of smoke, charred wood and damp. The odours had penetrated through the floorboards from the burned-out shell of the newspaper office downstairs and into the living quarters above.

Annie Burch tried to kill the smell by splashing some perfume around her room, but it was still there. The drapes were heavy with its pungency; her bedclothes, too. Perhaps she should move out to a hotel room, as Sheriff Kramer had suggested, but the living quarters had not suffered any actual damage and there were all her father's things to go through. It brought a lump to her throat and a sick feeling deep inside her, but there was no dodging the chore.

His clothes had to be sorted out and given away, instead of just being allowed to hang in the closet until they rotted. The printing machines could probably be salvaged, but she didn't know what to do about them. The banker had offered to try to sell them to the *Blall City Chronicle* – at a vastly reduced sum, of course, because of the fire damage, but she felt he only wanted to recoup some of the back payments owing on the mortgage.

She didn't understand how her father had fallen so far behind with the payments, but the banker had told her that Clive Burch had only been publishing the newspaper once a fortnight of late, instead of weekly as previously. It seemed he had been spending more and more time away in the County Seat and on other mysterious trips and had neglected his newspaper. Consequently, his income had fallen dramatically, and he had been unable to meet his mortgage payments.

Annie knew it wasn't like her father. The only thing that could keep him from publishing his paper on time was if he was caught up in some civic crusade that demanded all his attention. It had happened in the past, in other towns where he had published a newspaper. Twenty years earlier, Clive Burch had been known as something of a crusader but, after her mother had died, he had seemed to lose interest and had settled down into producing run-of-the-mill newspapers.

He had not bothered with any issues of great note for years, being content to go along at a steady pace, making a regular income in order to pay for her schooling and later, her further tuition to enable her to graduate as a school teacher.

Annie had graduated two years before and, after some initial uncertainty, had settled in to what she considered a good career. For the first time, she was independent, earning her own salary and not having to call on her father's funds any longer.

She sat bolt upright in the chair at the table where she was sorting through some of her father's papers as the thought hit her. Could that be it? Once she was truly independent of him, had he then turned to 'crusading' again – looking for some issue that would give him back his old fire and confidence and make the newspaper a truly great frontier journal?

Thinking about it further and remembering Reason's suggestion that perhaps someone had been hired to gun down her father, Annie Burch rose and hurried into her father's bedroom. She stood in the doorway, teeth tugging at her bottom lip, gaze moving slowly around the room, taking in the sparse furnishings, the clothes' closet, the leather-bound wooden trunk that contained his books, some historic issues of the newspaper and a lot of other papers.

There could be something in there, she thought. If he had been gathering information that would disclose any kind of scandal, he would hide the papers pertaining to it amongst a lot of other irrelevant material. He had told her once, that the best place to hide anything you didn't want found was in an obvious place. And that meant hiding information amongst other information.

She knelt before the trunk and slowly lifted the lid, wincing when she saw that it was literally overflowing with papers and books. It would take ages to sift through this …

'What about Reason Conant, in the meantime?' she murmured aloud. 'Even if I find something that would seem worth murdering for, there's nothing to prove it wasn't Conant I saw standing over Pa's body last night.'

She trembled a little, gripping the trunk lid tightly. There was very real doubt in her mind that it had been Reason Conant she had seen. The mental picture she had of the man who had shot at her was different, although she was unable to say exactly how. Reason Conant fitted the general description, but there were differences, and that story he had told, wild though it had sounded, could have been true.

There had been a note of sincerity in Conant's voice that had made her doubtful and she knew that young Cooper McCarty was also uncertain. Otherwise, he would never have agreed to her suggestion that he ride into the hills and try to find the cave the drifter had spoken of.

Annie gasped and jumped to her feet when she heard a sound in the doorway behind her. Ocie Kramer was standing there.

'What are you doing here?' she said, face pale.

He smiled crookedly. 'Sorry, Annie, didn't mean to startle you. I wanted to take another look around downstairs amongst the ashes and figured I'd let you know first – just in case you thought it was someone lootin' or somethin'.'

'Well, you certainly did startle me, Sheriff!' she said curtly, then turned and closed the lid of the trunk, which the lawman was staring at curiously. 'I-I guess you can go ahead, although I don't know what you expect to find.'

'Me, neither,' he admitted. 'Just thought there might be somethin' to shed more light on the whole loco business. That Clive's private papers? I mean his research stuff for the newspaper.'

'It's a mixture of junk and old editions he's kept over the years; some books he's read and re-read a hundred times, all riddled with worm now. In fact, I was just considering whether I'd simply make a bonfire out of the lot and save myself a lot of work,' Annie said.

'Well, yeah, that sounds like a good notion. Tell you what, Annie; we got us a big communal rubbish pit at the edge of town now. If you like, I could take that trunk out there and dump it in.'

Kramer tried not to sound too eager, but he saw by the look on her face that he hadn't succeeded and he inwardly cursed.

'Well, I haven't yet decided, Sheriff. Probably I'll rummage through it first. There might be something I will want to keep for sentimental reasons.'

'Sure,' he said, hoping he did a better job of keeping the disappointment out of his voice. He forced a grin. 'If you need a hand sortin' things out, just let me know, Annie. I'll be downstairs. By the way you seen Cooper McCarty lately?'

Looking uncomfortable, she said, 'Not for a little while, Sheriff. Is it important?'

Kramer was frowning as he stared at her coldly. 'Important enough. Want him to go up into the hills for me. Decided to check out that drifter's story about the cave.'

He broke off as Annie smiled in relief. 'Oh, that's all right then. Cooper has gone out to try to find the cave Conant spoke of. It was at my suggestion and I didn't want him to get into trouble. But if that's what you wanted him to do anyway …'

'Yes, sure,' Kramer said tightly. 'He should've checked with me first, though.'

Annie Burch looked a little abashed. 'I'm afraid I was a little insistent.'

The sheriff grunted. 'How long has he been gone?'

Annie shrugged. 'About an hour, I guess.'

Kramer smothered the curse that rose to his lips. If Cooper McCarty was already riding for the hills, the damned eager young beaver might well arrive back in town before the lynch party was over. He had better make sure Gideon Darrow sent in Powell and his hard cases right away. Then he remembered the other reason for visiting the girl.

'Aw, look, Annie, it bothers me some you livin' here after that fire – not to mention the murder. The floorboards might not be safe. Why don't you move into a hotel room for a spell? In fact, I have taken the liberty of bookin' you in – got you a front suite. You don't have to worry none; the town will pay. We thought a heap of your father and we would like to feel you're safe,' the sheriff said directly.

'Well, you did indeed take a liberty, Sheriff,' Annie told him coolly. 'Booking me in that way. But, thank you for your concern.'

'I'll give you a hand to pack a bag ...'

'You misunderstand, Sheriff. I'm grateful that you and the townsfolk have my interests at heart, but I don't intend to move from here.'

The sheriff looked taken aback. 'But the floor ain't safe!'

'Oh, but it is. Deputy McCarty tested it, scraped some of the boards and found they were only smoke-blackened. There is no real charring anywhere, as the fire was put out so swiftly and efficiently.'

'Good ol' Cooper,' growled Kramer, but forced a grin. 'Well, the suite's yours if you change your mind. And let me know if you want a hand sorting through all that stuff.' He gestured at the trunk, touched a hand to his hat brim and went out of the room, his forced smile disappearing abruptly.

Annie stared after him thoughtfully. She could swear Ocie Kramer was trying to push her out of here. And she was sure he had wanted to get a look at the papers in that trunk.

Could he be involved in her father's death? She shuddered at the thought.

She closed the door and bolted it before returning to kneel in front of the trunk. Then she lifted the lid and took out bundles of papers, beginning to get through them carefully.

The more she thought about Conant's suggestion, the more she felt he was right. Someone had hired a man to kill her father.

And she intended to find out who it was and why they had wanted her father dead. She had inherited a lot of Clive Burch's newspaperman's instincts.

CHAPTER 9

Isaac Powell was one of the toughest men in the territory. He had to be. He was foreman of the Rainbow Silver Mine Co. and needed hard fists to control the hard cases who worked for the company.

Powell was a beefy man with a big belly that strained at the brass-buckled worn leather belt he wore around his middle. That belt had been wrapped around his fist in many a brawl and the big buckle had mangled many an ear and torn open facial flesh. For Isaac Powell wasn't just tough, he was brutal – and he enjoyed it.

In the saloon bar, Conway dabbed at sweat on his upper lip as he stood at the bottom of the stairs leading to the floor above and watched the roughneck miners file through the bat-wing doors. Powell stood head and shoulders above the others, although they were all big men. Powell's bullet head was close-cropped and scarred from many past brawls. His face, too, showed the marks of fists, broken bottles and gun barrels. Not much more could happen to Isaac Powell's face and that was probably one reason why he was such a vicious fighter. He had taken just about every kind of punishment possible and was still able to come back for more. He had no looks to worry about spoiling and he could absorb blows that would incapacitate other men for a week.

Within twenty minutes of his arrival, Powell had knocked out two cowpokes from an outlying ranch, leaving them in bloody heaps against the wall. Then, sucking at a split knuckle, he turned to the room at large.

'By God, I wish them two rannies had been that son-of-a-gun they got locked up over there for Clive Burch's killin'! I'd like to break him into little pieces.' He held up his massive, brutal hands and everyone there had a mental picture of Powell literally breaking Reason Conant in two. 'Goddamn, I liked Burch. He ran a good newspaper, always gave the miners a fair shake. Don't seem right that some lousy drifter can come in here and blow him apart, then just sit snug and warm in a cell, waitin' in comfort while the law takes its sweet time.'

'Easy with that kind of talk, Isaac,' Alonzo Conway said quietly, but loud enough for everyone in the big barroom to hear. 'Sheriff's out of town and we don't want anything that sounds even remotely like lynch talk.'

Powell glared at Conway from under his scarred, beetling brows. 'Who asked you, beer puller? Button your lip or you'll be wearin' your nose on the back of your head. I'll say whatever I goddamn like and you won't stop me.'

Conway's look of concern wasn't all acting. He knew Powell was just as likely to turn on him if he felt like it, despite what Darrow would have told him about Conway's part in the lynch party.

'Sure, Isaac,' Conway told him swiftly. 'Just mentionin' it. Wouldn't want to see you fellers getting yourselves into

73

any trouble over a no-account like that Conant.'

Powell scowled into his glass and slammed it down on the counter. The barkeep hurried to refill it. The miner tossed down the drink, then snatched the bottle of whiskey from the barkeep's hand. The man glanced questioningly at Conway and seemed mighty relieved when the saloon keeper merely nodded permissively.

The foreman drank from the bottle, smacked his thick, misshapen lips and glared around the big, smoke-filled room.

'Well, you townsfolk gutless or what? Huh? I mean, I don't see you doin' nothin' about that varmint in the cell. You gonna let him sit there nice and snug, eatin' grub your taxes pay for, for maybe weeks until a circuit judge gets down here? Then we gotta foot the bill for a trial, when we already know the son of a bitch is guilty. Seems like one helluva waste of time and money to me. I damn well resent my taxes goin' to keep a lousy murderer like him out of the cold, while I gotta freeze my ass off to make enough to buy me a few drinks on a Saturday night.'

'You're right, Isaac,' roared another miner. 'Stinkin' murderin' scum sleepin' the days away, while honest men gotta work in this kinda weather. The hell of it is, he might get off, I hear. Ain't enough evidence that will stand up in court. Yet Ocie Kramer knows he's the killer and Annie Burch seen him.'

There was a murmur amongst the drinkers. Conway moved into the fray.

'That's right, gents, I'm afraid, but it's the price we pay under our legal system. Trouble is, it seems to work as well for the guilty as for the innocent,' Conway announced.

'I can deal out "justice" a damn sight quicker and cheaper than the courts!' growled Powell again swallowing a hefty slug from the whiskey bottle. 'At the end of a rope! I wouldn't be scared to tie the noose or haul that drifter up into the nearest cottonwood! No man worth his salt would turn away from such a chance.'

'Now, you best take it easy with that kind of talk, Isaac,' Alonzo Conway warned, sweating, hoping Powell wouldn't slug him just for the hell of it. 'That's mighty close to lynch talk.'

Isaac Powell glared at him, drank from the bottle, then looked around the room.

'So? Am I the only one who ain't afraid to put it into words? Truth is, if it be known, this whole damn town would like to see that drifter … Conant … hang for killin' poor Clive Burch.'

'Well, we ain't certain sure he done it, Isaac …' said one townsman uncomfortably, but he let his words trail off under Powell's steady, bleak stare.

'Well, Ocie Kramer's sure. He's the sheriff, ain't he? And his word's good enough for me,' Powell growled.

His fellow saloon patrons backed him on that and Powell smiled crookedly when he noticed a few of the townsmen joining in. It wouldn't be long before he had the whole room agreeing and then it was only a short step to the action itself.

He held the whiskey bottle high. 'Come on, fellers. This kind of thing's best talked about over a few drinks. Barkeeps! Set 'em up for the house. The drinks are on me!'

There was a surge of movement as men rushed for the bar and Isaac Powell stood back, bottle tilted against his mouth, beady eyes seeking Alonzo Conway.

The saloon keeper nodded in slow approval.

The lynch party was under way.

Although it was only mid-afternoon, there was a dusk-like gloom over Biggs. In some stores, a few lamps had been lit in an effort to dispel the shadows. The wind still howled, although the snow wasn't falling as heavily. But it was a miserable, bitter day to be out and Cooper McCarty was mighty glad to ride his steaming mount back into town and turn it over to the complaining liveryman.

He turned a deaf ear to the man's complaints and, tugging his collar up higher about his ears, took his gunnysack from his saddle horn and hurried out of the stables. The streets were practically deserted and he smiled as he heard loud laughter and drunken songs coming from the saloon. That was the best place to be on a day like this, he thought. He ducked his head as the wind shrieked about him and so missed hearing Isaac Powell's voice whipping up the drinkers in the saloon towards a fever pitch.

McCarty went to the law office and was surprised when he didn't find Sheriff Kramer there. He went through to the cellblock. Reason Conant, who was lying on the bunk, sat up as the deputy approached.

'How about some grub or hot coffee?' the drifter asked. 'I'm starved.'

'Thought the sheriff would have taken care of that by now, but I will see to it directly.' McCarty opened his gunnysack and showed Reason the contents. 'I found your cave, mister, and the saddlebags and canteen of sand you mentioned.'

76

Reason looked quickly at the deputy's pinched, cold face.

'You went out into the hills in this blizzard to check my story?' he asked incredulously.

McCarty shrugged. 'Annie Burch sort of talked me into it and it ain't snowin' quite so hard right now. Point is, you were tellin' the truth, it seems. I mean, I found your camp and looked for this feller's body ...'

'Lannan,' put in Reason automatically, wondering why the deputy frowned and looked at him closely before he continued.

'But I guess he was too deep under. Couldn't locate him. How did you know his name was Lannan? Weren't nothin' in the saddlebags with that name on it.'

'The sheriff mentioned it,' explained Reason.

'He did? Well, that's funny. He never told me about any Lannan. And how would he know, anyway?' The deputy was perplexed.

Reason Conant shrugged. 'Maybe he recognized him when he shot his horse last night. He could have meant Gus Lannan, the gunfighter and hired killer.'

'Huh-huh,' agreed McCarty slowly. 'But the sheriff made a point of tellin' us he wouldn't recognize the man again 'cause he only seen his back ...' He seemed to stir himself abruptly. 'Anyways, it don't much matter who it was, long as it proves your story. 'Course, findin' these here saddlebags and canteen don't necessarily mean you are off the hook, but they show you was tellin' the truth about somethin'.'

Reason regarded him soberly. 'I spoke gospel all down the line, McCarty. It happened just the way I said. I wish to hell you had dug a little deeper in that snow and brought in Lannan's body.'

'There's that name again.' McCarty closed the gunny-sack and hefted it. 'Well, I got some visitin' to do. I'll get you somethin' hot to eat and drink directly, Conant.'

'Thanks, Deputy. I'm much obliged to you for going to all that trouble.'

Cooper McCarty looked both pleased and slightly embarrassed. 'Hell, it's only what any good lawman would do.'

As McCarty went out the door, Reason raised his voice and called, 'Yeah. What any good lawman would.'

The door stayed slightly ajar for a moment, as though McCarty had paused to consider his words, then closed firmly. There was no sound of the key turning in the lock this time, and Reason, feeling better now, began pacing the cell floor in an attempt to ward off the chill that was creeping into his bones.

CHAPTER 10

'Then it seems the drifter was telling the truth, after all,' said Annie Burch as she looked at the saddlebags and canteen in McCarty's gunnysack. She lifted her gaze to the deputy's flushed face. 'Have you shown these to Sheriff Kramer yet?'

McCarty shook his head. 'Went looking for him, but they tell me there was some kind of fight up at the mine. A man was killed and the sheriff had to go and look into it.' He frowned. 'He ought to have deputized someone to watch over the jail, but seems he didn't. He just hightailed it as soon as Darrow sent in word. Saloon's full of miners, swillin' booze. They were makin' a racket till I showed up, then they all went quiet. I thought they looked kind of guilty, matter of fact … There were some townsfolk, too – all pretty drunk. Seemed mighty surprised to see me.'

'You sound worried, Coop. Is there something you want to tell me?' She pressed.

'Uh-no, I guess not. Being stupid, I suppose,' he said reluctantly.

'Coop, tell me. I know that look. Something's on your mind.'

He shifted his feet uncomfortably. 'Well, I might be overly suspicious, Annie, but it seems mighty strange that Sheriff Kramer would leave the jail unguarded and just take off for the mines. I know Darrow's a powerful man hereabouts, but he never carried much weight with Kramer. And those fellers were boozin' it up in the saloon and … Well I ain't sure, but I thought one of 'em had a rope which he got out of sight fast when I went in.' He paused and frowned worriedly. 'I only thought about all these things after I'd left the saloon and was on my way over here.'

Annie sucked in a sharp breath. 'You're not saying that's a lynch party forming in the saloon, Coop?'

The young deputy squirmed. 'I just dunno, Annie. And, fact is, I ain't sure what to do about it. But I guess I better get back to the jail pronto.'

'Yes, you better had,' the girl said tensely. She seemed to be trying to make up her mind about something. Suddenly she signed for McCarty to wait, then took something from under a cloth on the parlour table.

It was a black Morocco-bound book with brass corners and a brass filigreed lock. McCarty looked at her questioningly.

'I found this amongst my father's papers,' she said. 'Conant suggested that my father might have been killed because he was working on some kind of crusade. I guess Conant didn't realize that, some years ago, my father was a dedicated crusader against corruption and crime. He had quietened down over the past few years but had never really changed.' She tapped the book, face pale now. 'There are notes in here concerning Gideon Darrow, Alonzo Conway and Ocie Kramer. It seems my father had proof that they have been swindling the mine of thousands of dollars, using the money to buy up land under false names, then re-selling it at enormous profits to a railroad company that is expanding in this direction.'

'Holy smoke, Annie!' Cooper McCarty breathed, grey faced.

'It-it's motive enough for murder and I knew my father well enough not to doubt anything he documented like this. He was very thorough and never committed word to paper unless he was sure of his facts,' Annie said sternly.

'Then if the sheriff is mixed up in … What's that?'

McCarty broke off and lunged for the window, pulling the drapes apart. Annie heard him curse, although he tried hard to smother it. Over his shoulder, she saw the drunken mob boiling out of the saloon and there was no mistaking their intention. Big Isaac Powell held a coiled rope, knotted in a hangman's noose, in his brutal hands as he led the mob down the street towards the jailhouse.

'They're gonna lynch Conant!' McCarty breathed, wild-eyed.

Annie grabbed him swiftly. 'Coop, you have to get him out! This is no time to worry about the whys and wherefores of his guilt or innocence. You have to get him out before that mob lynches him! You know why Kramer left town. He was going to send you out, too, only you had already gone.' She urged him towards the door. 'Coop, slip out the back way and get to the jailhouse as fast as you can. I will saddle horses and meet you behind the jail building. We will try to get to Blall City.'

He blinked. 'Blall City? "We"? You mean you are coming too?'

Annie nodded, grimly. 'I have to get this book to the US Marshal there. Now go, Coop! Before it's too late for Conant!'

Reason Conant had heard the sounds of a lynch mob before. Twice, as a matter of fact. But this was the first time he knew the mob was coming for him.

It wasn't a good feeling. It made his stomach swirl and bile rise in this throat.

The animal sounds filtered through the high, barred window. He listened briefly and his heart hammered as he identified the growling and cursing of drunken men working themselves up to a killing pitch. He stood on the bunk and jumped for the bars. With his hands gripping the freezing iron, he drew himself up and pressed his face to the opening. The wind slashed at him and his eyes watered almost instantly, but not before he had glimpsed the determined mob crossing the end of the lane. Then a swirl of snow hid them from his sight and he dropped back to the bunk and looked wildly around towards the cell passage. He stiffened when he heard a door bang open and the brief howl of the wind.

Deputy Cooper McCarty come into the passage from the side door then hurriedly closed it again and barred it. He turned, wiping snow and sleet from his face as Reason shook the bars.

'Get me out of here, Deputy!' he pleaded.

McCarty held up his hand then started towards the door leading to the front office. 'I need the keys. You hear them?'

'Yeah, got a glimpse of the mob. Hurry, don't waste your time asking me questions.'

The deputy disappeared into the office and as he came back, there was a chorus of wild yells from out front and fists banged on the street doors. The deputy hesitated, then stooped and skidded the key ring along the floor towards Reason's cell. It came to a halt just outside the barred door.

'Let yourself out and try to get the yard door open,' the young deputy snapped, pointing to the heavy, iron-bound door at the far end of the passage. It was padlocked from the inside. 'Key's on there somewhere.'

Glass shattered in the office and Cooper McCarty leapt back, pulling the door closed. Reason strained to reach the keys through the bars, just managing to hook the ring with his fingertips. He drew them towards him and swore when he saw how many keys dangled from the big ring. There must be a dozen at least. He knew the longest and heaviest was for the cell door, but he also knew he was going to waste considerable time trying to find the right key for the padlock on the yard door.

There was shouting in the front office as he awkwardly pushed the big key into the cell door lock and twisted it. He recognized McCarty's voice amongst the other, harsher ones. Then the key turned in the lock and he threw his weight against the barred door, as a racket of gunfire erupted from the front office. Reason burst out into the passage, snatched the keys from the lock, and then glanced at the yard door and the number of keys on the ring. He shook his head and ran for the door leading to the front office. It opened before he got there and McCarty backed into the passage crouching, snapping two shots back into the office. His face was pale as he glanced over his shoulder.

'Get that other door opened!' he hissed.

'You do it! I will waste too much time trying to find the right key.' Reason tossed the ring at the deputy and McCarty instinctively caught it. 'I'll get my gun rig,' Reason said.

'No!' Cooper McCarty snapped, his smoking Colt swinging to cover the prisoner. From beyond the door came more shots and the woodwork rattled and shuddered as bullets struck home. The deputy shook his head swiftly. 'I ain't goin' so far as to arm you.'

'The hell with you, Deputy!' Reason Conant said and swept the six-gun aside with his left hand. 'Sorry about this.' He followed through with his right, hitting McCarty hard enough to send him sprawling, then wrenched open the door and dived through at floor level. He glimpsed men at the smashed window. They pushed guns between the bars and fired at him as he rolled behind the heavy roll-top desk. He began wrenching open the drawers.

'There's the murderin', no-good drifter!' someone yelled.

'McCarty's let the son of a bitch out!' shouted Isaac Powell. 'Get around back! They'll try to go out that way!'

Reason hoped the deputy had enough sense to get the padlock open while he was searching for his gun rig. He found it, at last, in the second top drawer. He snatched it and grabbed a carton of shells at the same time. Splinters flew as a fusillade of bullets raked the desk. He started to roll back towards the passage door, but lead tore up the floorboards and he jerked back behind the desk, cursing. If they kept him pinned down, he would be a dead duck. He was a fool for coming after his gun, but he hadn't wanted to face a bloodthirsty lynch mob with only his bare hands.

The gun cabinet was on the wall above him. Bullets had already shattered the glass doors. There were several rifles and two double-barrelled shotguns there. Reason wrenched open the bottom drawer, where he had seen cartons of shotgun shells only seconds earlier. He snatched one, then lunged up and grabbed a Greener from the cabinet, slicing his wrist and hand on the jagged glass. The guns at the window blasted, but a second too late.

'He's got a Greener!' someone yelled and as Reason thrust two shells into the breach, he heard boots scrabbling on the porch.

He cocked the hammers and threw the gun across the desk, not even bothering to sight on the window as he pulled a trigger. The Greener blasted and rose off the desk in recoil, filling the room with thunder. The window frame disintegrated, men screamed and scattered and he saw some cut down like wheat under a scythe.

Reason Conant rose to his feet and lunged for the passage door, firing the second barrel into the street door. The buckshot ripped through the panels, leaving a jagged hole and bringing more wild yells and screams of agony from outside. Then Reason was through the passage. McCarty, who had just opened the padlock on the yard door, turned his pale face towards him.

'Some of them went around here!' Reason panted, as he shoved fresh loads into the Greener. 'Better let me go first.'

The deputy seemed about to argue, but Reason shouldered him aside and wrenched open the door, leaping through with the shotgun butt braced on his hip. There were six or seven armed men leaping over the side fence, dropping into the yard and charging towards the cellblock. Two began firing as soon as they saw Reason. He fired one barrel and saw a man hurled through the air as the shot struck him. Another man's legs were cut from under him and he fell screaming. The others turned and leapt wildly over the fence, hurling themselves over the palings and sprawling in the alley beyond. Reason hurried them along by discharging the second barrel, which chewed a large chunk out of the top of the fence. He dropped the Greener, took his gun rig down from where it was slung over his shoulder and buckled it around the outside of his jacket. McCarty ran up, grabbed his arm and pointed up the yard towards the rear fence where there was a gate behind overgrown weeds and piles of rubbish.

'Mounts!' McCarty panted and took off, urging Reason along.

There were sounds back in the jailhouse that warned Reason the mob was breaking its way in from the street. He pounded after the deputy who was already kicking open the rickety gate and stumbling out into the slushy lane beyond. As Reason ran through after him, he was surprised to see Annie Burch, white as the swirling snow, sitting a prancing mount and holding the reins of two others.

She didn't speak as she thrust the reins into his hands. He flung himself into the saddle. McCarty was already up and spinning his horse.

As the three rode hard for the end of the laneway, the lynch mob surged out of the jail building into the yard and guns hammered, the bullets whining over the fugitives' heads.

'Get after them!' Isaac Powell bawled, wiping snow from his eyes, his voice hoarse and savagely angry. 'Get after them and we'll string them all up together!'

The mob, blood lust at its peak, yelled their agreement and began to disperse in search of mounts.

CHAPTER 11

Guns blazed behind as the three fugitives ran their mounts on into the thickening gloom of the afternoon.

They cast frequent glances behind for the first mile or so, then they were well past the last houses and the town dropped swiftly from sight. The girl had taken the lead and McCarty and Reason followed without question, but when they were into the foothills and it was almost full dark, she reined down and waited for them to draw alongside.

Annie was dressed for the cold in a fur jacket, lined jodhpurs, gloves, woollen muffler and a close-fitting fur hat, which covered her flaxen hair, and had flaps to protect her ears. Even in this emergency, Reason thought, she made a fine-looking picture sitting the prancing, snorting mount.

'Do you think they are coming after us?' she panted.

'Hell, most likely they will,' said Reason. 'That big hombre with the smashed face was yelling at the others to get horses when we cleared that lane.'

'What're your plans, Annie?' McCarty asked, turning to the girl. Then, as Reason, too, instinctively looked towards the girl, the deputy whipped out his Colt and pointed it at him. 'I'll take that six-gun now, Conant!'

The drifter was caught off-guard and he cursed himself for falling for the lawman's trick, but made no effort to unbuckle his gun belt. He folded his hands on the saddle horn and looked into Cooper McCarty's face with narrowed eyes.

'You want it, you take it, Deputy,' Reason challenged.

The girl was alarmed, as she glanced from one to the other. 'What is this? We don't have time for this sort of thing, Coop!'

''Course we don't,' Reason agreed. 'That mob will be along directly and all our running will have been for nothing if we don't get moving.'

'No!' Cooper McCarty said stubbornly. 'I let you out to save your neck, but that don't mean you get your gun back. You got a good chance of bein' innocent, but we'll let the US Marshal in Blall City decide that, I reckon.'

'You blamed fool!' Reason Conant told him crisply. 'If I hadn't grabbed my gun and that Greener, we would both be dead men by now. You would have been blown apart or swinging from a cottonwood right alongside me.'

'That's as maybe, but I wanted to try to get you out of town without bloodshed and you downed several of them miners and townsmen,' McCarty noted.

Reason snorted. 'They were gonna lynch me, goddamn it! What would you expect me to do?'

'You should've gotten that rear door open, like I said, while I held them off ...'

Suddenly, Reason kicked his heels into his mount and the startled animal emitted a shrill whinny and leapt forward. It slammed into the deputy's mount and

McCarty grabbed for the saddle horn while Reason ducked and reached for the deputy's six-gun. However, it exploded in a wild shot before he could close his hand around it. He cursed and drew his own Colt, clipping McCarty lightly on the head with the barrel. He reeled, but Reason caught him and steadied him, then rammed his gun muzzle under the deputy's chin.

'We don't have time for arguing, damn you! Savvy?' He twisted the barrel hard and McCarty, eyes bulging, nodded. Reason flicked his glaze to the tight-faced girl. 'You have someplace in mind for us to go, ma'am? Or are you leaving us here?'

Annie swiftly shook her head. 'No, I'm coming too. We have to get to Blall City. I found a kind of journal belonging to my father. It appears he had some sort of proof that Sheriff Kramer, Alonzo Conway, the saloon owner, and Gideon Darrow, manager of the silver mine, were involved in a scandal and fraud. I believe it's why he was killed, and it would seem those three were behind his murder. They are the most powerful men in Biggs. That's why I have to get the book to a Federal Marshal.'

'Leaves you, Deputy,' Reason told McCarty. 'You hankerin' to come along or do we part company here?'

'You're still my prisoner!' the deputy gritted stubbornly.

'He'll get us killed,' Reason told the girl. 'I owe him something so I'm kinda reluctant to slug him and let him take his chances, but if he comes, he is going to be a nuisance.'

'We have to take Coop with us!' Annie exclaimed. 'It's unthinkable that we leave him.'

Reason shrugged. 'Well, you will have to lead on,

ma'am. This is all strange territory to me and I reckon if we don't move, we will either freeze or that mob will come riding out of that wall of snow yonder.' He gestured down the trail leading back towards town. Then he put his cold gaze on McCarty. 'You gonna behave?'

Cooper McCarty hesitated, then nodded curtly. 'You just stay close and don't be so quick to use that gun of yours.'

Reason chuckled and gestured for the deputy to put away his Colt. When he had done so, he holstered his gun. Suddenly, he cocked his head to one side.

'Horses! Which way, ma'am?'

For a moment, Annie looked uncertain. Then she pointed to her left and urged her mount in that direction. Reason Conant followed the girl and they raced into a draw that was thick underfoot with piled snow. He hipped in the saddle and saw McCarty behind him and as the horses' hooves crunched lightly on the powdery snow, he heard again the thundering clatter of pursuit along the trail.

They were not quite fast enough to get out of sight. There was still sufficient light for Powell and the drunk blood-crazed townsmen and hard case miners to see the trail left by the fugitives' mounts. Powell pointed triumphantly and, waving the rifle that seemed little more than a toy in his massive fist, led the posse into the draw.

'They they go!' he yelled, catching a glimpse of the trio as they set their horses up the slope. He brought the rifle to his shoulder and fired, levered and fired three more fast shots. The thunder of the gunfire reverberated up the draw and snow exploded from the rim rock close to the hooves of McCarty's mount. The animal reared and almost went over the edge, but the deputy hauled it back with brute force and spurred it up the slope.

Reason's Colt bucked and roared in his fist as he fired down into the draw. He threw a swift glance in McCarty's direction. 'Get the drift now, Deputy? They aim to kill all of us, not just me!'

McCarty said nothing, but he drew his gun and snapped two shots into the draw as a ragged volley of gunfire came from down there. Bullets zipped into the snow and struck sparks from an outcrop of granite. Annie cried out in alarm as her horse pranced and plunged.

'Keep going!' snapped Reason, firing downslope again. 'Get as high as you can. They're dismounting for a better shot at us!'

He emptied his Colt, wheeled his mount and jammed his heels hard in the horse's sides, yelling as he urged the animal up the slope. McCarty fired his last two shots and trailed after him, the mounts head-to-rump. Both men hunched low over their horses' necks as the posse in the draw tried to get them in their sights. But the wind was stronger up here and it lifted the snow in blinding white swirls, which flew between the fugitives and the posse.

Isaac Powell and his men cut loose with volley after volley, but they didn't get a clear view of the fugitives again. Cursing, the battered miner clambered back onto his mount as the echoes of the gunfire died away.

'Save your lead!' he bawled. 'Snow's hid 'em. We will catch up with them if we get movin' now. Come on! Move, all of you! I still got that hangman's noose ready for 'em!'

The men cheered, mounted again and yelled wildly as Powell led them through the draw and onto the slopes of the mountain. By now it was full dark and the wind was increasing in intensity and Powell's confidence ebbed when he saw the snow sweeping down the peaks. It seemed the weather was going to help McCarty, Conant and the girl, not the posse.

'Faster! Move!' Isaac Powell roared desperately, lashing and kicking at his own unfortunate mount. 'Faster or they'll get away, damn it!'

The men in the posse drove their mounts brutally and passed around the bottles of whiskey they had brought with them to ward off the bitter cold. A couple of men were so drunk that they simply tumbled out of their saddles and sprawled in the snow. The others laughed and rode on. Powell's lips tightened and he cursed.

He had misjudged a few things, it seemed. He had allowed the mob to get a mite too drunk and he had been a little late in getting to the jailhouse. If he had been only five minutes earlier, he would have arrived before the deputy, and Reason would now be swinging from the cottonwood in Main Street. He had also misjudged the weather. It had looked like clearing a little. The blizzard had dropped to intermittent gusts when they had left town, and he had figured his drink-crazed mob would easily run down the fugitives.

But the damn snow had slowed them down, hidden their quarry and even obscured their tracks in places. Now it looked as though the visibility on the side of the mountain was almost non-existent.

Isaac Powell wasn't looking forward to reporting to Darrow and Kramer. What made it even harder was the fact that he had never before had to report failure to carry out a task. So he decided to make one more effort, before quitting.

Riding back amongst the drunken posse, he used his hands and tongue, trying to keep the booze-ridden riders going. He shook some of them violently, pushing two right off their mounts. He roared and raved, then pointed across the slope and told them to keep going – he wanted the fugitives run down tonight.

But it was no good. Powell knew that, even before he had finished cuffing the last of the drunken posse men. The wind was stronger and the snow gusts were thicker, colder and more violent. The fugitives' tracks would be obscured and the posse had lost sight of them after they had crossed the rim rock.

But Powell was damned if he was going to make it easy for these fools. He figured they had let him down. He rode amongst his miners, only three of whom were too drunk to be of any use, and raked them with his hard, beady eyes.

'I'm goin' back to the mine,' he announced. 'I'll have to tell Mr Darrow what has happened. Now, these here townsmen are gonna be out of booze soon and when they sober up, they will want to head back to their snug beds. Well, don't let them. Make the bastards stay out here tonight. Let 'em freeze their asses off. I don't care what they do come mornin', out in the open. Savvy?'

'Hell, Ike, that means we gotta do the same thing,' one miner protested, but swiftly raised his hands in a placating gesture when he saw the look on Powell's face. 'OK, OK, I guess the extra pay we have promised takes care of that.'

Powell nodded unsmilingly. 'I'll be back at daylight and I want to find you all here, understand?'

He raked his chill gaze around them once more to

emphasize the unspoken threat, then nodded curtly, wheeled his mount and started back down the snow-covered slopes, hoping he could find the trail back to town in the howling blizzard.

The only compensation was that he knew Reason Conant and the others would be suffering because of it, too.

CHAPTER 12

'Hell almighty! You tellin' me that Conant's runnin' loose somewhere in the hills with that loco deputy and the gal?'

Gideon Darrow arched his eyebrows as Sheriff Ocie Kramer vented his wrath on Powell. The big mine manager dropped his feet to the floor from where he had them propped on the desk and sat up straight. He saw Powell watching him: the foreman didn't give a damn about Kramer's raving and ranting, but he was concerned about how the mine manager was going to react.

'That lousy, stupid deputy!' rasped the sheriff, face dark with the anger boiling within him. 'If he hadn't been such a damn eager beaver and gone out to look for that cave, he wouldn't have been back in town until Conant had been strung up! The gal talked him into it!'

Darrow motioned Kramer to silence. 'Save your breath, Ocie. No use your shootin' your mouth off. What's done is done. And it seems you didn't take my advice and deputize a townsman to guard the jail while you rode out here to investigate the fake brawl I organized.'

Kramer scowled at the mine manager. 'I forgot!' he growled. 'Plumb forgot. I was eager to quit town, and when your men rode in I was still thinkin' about the gal and that trunk full of Clive Burch's papers. I just high-tailed it out here ...' He rounded abruptly on Powell, frowning. 'You say Annie went with Cooper and the drifter?'

'She sure did. She had the horses waiting for them behind the jail and led those fellers into the hills herself.'

Sheriff Kramer ripped out an obscene curse. 'You know what is happening, don't you? She has found Clive's damn diary, or journal, or whatever you call it, in that trunk. Soon as I saw it I had a hunch that is where he would have stashed the book.'

'Then you should have insisted you go through it with her, right there and then,' Darrow said.

Kramer gave him a hard look. 'I wasn't sure how hard to push the gal. I still thought there might be a chance of getting her out of the place and into the hotel, so we could go through the joint ourselves,' he tried to explain.

Gideon Darrow grunted his displeasure with the explanation. 'I'm inclined to agree with you, Ocie, that she has found the book. She is likely taking it to the marshal in Blall City.'

'Then, by God, she has to be stopped!' Kramer snapped.

'That much is obvious,' growled the mine manager. 'Isaac, those townsmen won't be much use to us, come morning. They will be hungover and they will have lost their urge to lynch the drifter. So how many men does that leave you with?'

'Took down nine, but two or three of 'em drank more than they was supposed to, and they'll be hungover to hell and back, come mornin'. I'd say we will have about six useful men we could call on,' Powell said, his face showing his frustration in sorting it all out.

'Need more than that,' growled Kramer. 'If they get deep into them hills we could lose them for good.'

'We will have more,' Darrow said calmly, getting to his feet. He went to a wooden cabinet and opened the door with a small key he kept on his watch chain. He took out a cartridge belt with a holstered Colt attached. Kramer could see two polished and oiled Winchesters still in their racks in the cupboard. As Darrow buckled on the gun rig he said, 'There will be ten of us. That ought to do it.'

'Ten?' blinked the sheriff.

Gideon Darrow took down one rifle and examined it briefly, working the oiled lever and hammer expertly. The action operated smoothly, but the mine manager shook his head briefly, replaced the rifle and took down the second one. He tried the action of this, too, and it seemed to satisfy him, for he pocketed two boxes of cartridges, closed the cupboard and turned to the sheriff.

'Yes, ten of us, Ocie. Isaac and his six good miners, you, me and Alonzo Conway,' Darrow said coolly.

The sheriff frowned even deeper. 'You and Conway comin' along on the manhunt?' he asked incredulously.

Darrow smiled crookedly. 'Why not, Ocie? It would appear to be in our best interests.' His eyes and voice hardened as he looked coldly at Powell. 'Seeing as things have been fouled up so far.'

The big foreman flushed and dropped his gaze, moving his huge feet in their wet, hobnailed boots uncomfortably. Kramer raised his eyebrows slightly. He had never before seen Isaac Powell squirm in front of any man, for any reason, and he knew he was witnessing a rare occurrence. He revised his opinion of Darrow; any man who could throw a scare into Powell and make him feel uneasy deserved respect – of that he was certain.

'We provision ourselves for a week in the wild, gentlemen,' the mine manager went on. 'And we stay out until we run them to ground. We kill all three, but the gal isn't to die until we have the book. Savvy?'

'Makes sense,' admitted the sheriff. 'But I dunno whether Alonzo will come along. He ain't much of an outdoorsman.'

Darrow smiled thinly. 'He will come. It is in his interests, too. I will insist that he join us.' His smile widened and he winked ponderously at Powell. The foreman's battered face brightened. He looked like a cur dog, suddenly hearing a kind word after being in its master's bad books. 'Isaac, you organize the stores, pack mules and horses. Ocie, you and me had better study the survey map and see which trails they are likely to use.'

'They might hole up,' the sheriff opined. 'Dunno about the gal, 'cause she's been away for a spell, but Cooper McCarty's got friends in them hills; friends who would hide 'em out till we get tired of looking.'

Gideon Darrow's rocky face was hard now. 'Then we look up these friends of McCarty's and either make them our friends, or throw such a scare into them that they won't let the deputy and his friends within ten miles of their spreads.'

Ocie Kramer whistled softly. 'Playin' rough, this time, are we?'

Darrow's cold eyes drilled into the sheriff's face. 'As

rough as we need to get – and then some. You know, as well as I do, that we are finished unless we get our hands on that book before the US Marshal does.'

Kramer knew there was no point in arguing with that.

The fugitives spent the night in an abandoned way station beside the old stage trail that had wound through the hills before the coming of the railroad. They could not risk a fire, but the girl had brought plenty of blankets and they all huddled together in one corner, under a fallen section of roof, feeling its weight gradually increase as snow piled up on it.

While the storm lashed the hills, Reason figured they had little to worry about from the posse. But when, sometime after midnight, the wind dropped and the snow diminished to intermittent spatters, he figured the dawn might bring more danger than any of them anticipated.

It was a beautiful, crisp mountain morning, the hills carpeted with glistening white snow, the trees around the tumbledown, picturesque old way station bending under its weight. Reason looked over the country from the doorway as he buckled on his gun rig.

'Don't light a fire,' he told the girl as he saw her gathering sticks and leaves.

Annie looked at him in surprise. 'We will need hot coffee and food.'

'Sure would be good,' he agreed. 'But there's no wind. It's almighty still out there. Even a wisp of smoke will be seen miles away and it will rise straight up, pinpointing our position.'

She nodded slowly and dumped the kindling she had gathered.

'It is very cold. We will just have to have hardtack washed down with water,' Reason offered.

Just then, Cooper McCarty came back from checking the horses, rubbing his hands briskly. 'What's for breakfast?' he asked eagerly, hungrily.

'Hardtack and water,' Reason replied firmly.

As the deputy blinked, Annie explained Reason's precautions and the deputy nodded in reluctant agreement. 'Yeah. Guess you're right. Of course, there may not be a posse left by now. There were mostly drunk and they will be mighty hungover this morning. Most of them will want to get back to their homes – if they didn't return home last night.'

Reason stared at him. 'You want to risk that?'

McCarty held his gaze briefly, then looked away. 'Nope. Guess not.'

'There is more to this now, than just a lynching,' Reason Conant reminded the lawman. 'The necktie party was supposed to be a kind of red herring, to involve the townsfolk in something outside the law. It would have helped in the future, if there had been any kind of leak about the fraud Darrow, Conway and the sheriff were mixed up in.' He turned to the girl. 'You were gonna tell me more about that.'

Annie Burch looked uncertain. 'Well, is this the time and place for all that? I mean ...'

'You're right. We ought to be on the trail.'

'And we are gonna leave tracks a blind man could follow,' Cooper McCarty said with bitterness. 'I swear I would rather that damn wind was still howling.'

'Yeah. If they are coming at all, they are going to have an easy time tracking us,' Reason admitted. 'Where we headed? I don't even know where this Blall City is.'

'Over yonder. But through miles of hills,' replied the young deputy. 'We can't take the normal trail that skirts the mountains, of course. But I know some old trappers' trails in there that will get us to where we want to go.'

'The sheriff know them trails too?' asked Reason.

'Guess he does.'

'We – we might not have enough food to stay in the mountains more than a couple of days, Coop,' Annie Burch told the lawman. 'I didn't have time to do more than throw what I could lay my hands on into a couple of gunnysacks.'

'We will manage,' Reason said. When she looked dubious, he smiled faintly. 'I'm a drifter, ma'am – used to riding with my belt pulled to the last notch. We can't hunt with guns, of course, but I can trap animals. And, anyways, there must be folks living in there, where we could get some extra grub.'

'Sure. There are spreads,' agreed McCarty. 'I know a few folk living in the hills who might help us out. In fact, I know some who most definitely would.'

'Kramer likely knows them, too, I guess,' opined Reason.

McCarty looked thoughtful. 'Well, he knows my kin, but I didn't aim to go near them. He knows the Kirks and the Claybergs I went to school with, but I don't think he knows anything about the Widow Young and her son, Chet. I got sort of friendly with him and his mother after old man Young got himself gored to death out on the Teton Rim, when he was riding trail herd. I had to take the news to them. They was doing kind of poorly at the time because Chet was just recovering from pneumonia, so I went out a few times, on my days off, and did some chores for them. Me and Chet get along fine and the widow is mighty grateful too. She would give us some grub, I reckon.'

'If she has been living in the hills for a spell, she might know a good place where we could hole up,' Reason said, his words causing the others to look at him sharply. 'Well, figure it out. Kramer and his posse have got to stop us. They will realize by now you have found your father's book, Annie. They have got to stop us getting to the marshal in Blall City. They will send someone ahead to watch for us, so it would be crazy to go straight there, even through hidden trails in the hills. We had best lie low for a while, until they get nervous and figure we might have cut away to the south and headed for Salt Lake City, or even taken the trail to Cheyenne. We won't need to hole up for long. A week ought to do it. Then they will start scattering all over the countryside, trying to figure out where we have gone.'

'That sounds like a good idea, Mr Conant,' Annie Burch said.

'Call me Reason,' he said.

Annie continued after acknowledging him with a nod, 'But I don't like the thought of a week in these hills, at this time of year. The blizzards will be back in another day or so. They could even close in again in a few hours.'

'We will need somewhere snug,' Reason said, 'I didn't mean to camp out. That is why I figured this Widow Young just might know the right place for us to hole up for a stretch.'

'Well that sounds great, but first we have to get out of here,' the young deputy said, a little impatiently, looking out at the expanse of virgin snow glittering in the bright sunlight. 'And we got to be sure that the posse doesn't trail us, which is sure gonna be some chore.'

'Yeah, you are right about that, we better move. Once we are in the timber we will have a better chance of covering our trail.'

They broke camp swiftly and didn't bother trying to conceal the fact that they had spent the night there. As Reason pointed out, there was little point in it, when the old way station was the only possible shelter they could have used in this neck of the woods. Their tracks showed plainly in the snow, angling up the slope and into a stand of timber. The posse would have an easy trail to follow, at least as far as the trees.

Once in the thick timber, Reason sent the others ahead, asking Annie to try to walk her horse as closely as possible to Cooper's mount.

Reason himself stopped his mount beneath the low branches of the trees, which were sagging under the weight of snow that had been deposited on them by the storm. He used the old mountain man's trick of scooping snow from the branches and dumping it into the tracks made by the horses.

Of course, it was a slow process and Reason lagged way behind the others as he slowly worked his way up through the trees. But they waited for him on a ridge, and when he caught up to them, he grinned at the girl and wiped powdery snow from his face.

'So far so good,' he announced.

'Sure,' agreed Cooper McCarty. Then he pointed down the far side of the ridge. 'How are we going to get down there without leaving a trail? Fly?'

Reason Conant felt his face stiffen as he looked out over the miles of virgin snow, unbroken by a rock or tree for several miles.

'All that posse has to do is ride up through the timber without even bothering to search for our tracks amongst the trees – 'cause once they look down onto that slope, they will see where we have gone, just as if we had pointed the way! All your efforts have been for nothing! What do you have to say about that?'

The drifter gave the deputy a hard look, hearing the bitterness in his voice and knowing the lawman was still unhappy about Reason retaining his gun and assuming command. But it had just worked out in that manner.

During the night, Reason had thought about riding out on his own and making his escape. If the girl hadn't been involved, he might have done just that. The book she was carrying meant Kramer and his co-conspirators would try to kill her – and whoever was with her. The point was, she had gone out on a limb for him, risked her neck to get him away from the lynch mob, as had Cooper McCarty. And he was obliged to stay and see this through.

'Aren't we sort of exposed here?' Annie asked abruptly, sweeping a hand around the high ridge.

'Yeah, we could be,' admitted Reason. 'That slope's a death trap for us. We will do better riding the ridge.'

'We will be skylined if we stick to the ridge!' protested McCarty.

Reason pointed to grey splashes of partially-covered rocks on either side of the ridge spine, which were too steep and smooth to retain the snow. 'We will make use of them rocks as much as possible, and we will be just below the top of the ridge. If we ride hunched over, we shouldn't skyline ourselves.'

McCarty was sceptical and, in truth, so too was Reason, but they had few options available to them, so they urged their mounts forward. The drifter again brought up the rear, using a branch he had brought from the timber to sweep loose snow over the tracks.

He knew it wouldn't fool an experienced man tracker for long.

He just hoped it would long enough.

CHAPTER 13

Alonzo Conway resented being dragged along on this chase through the freezing hills and he let Kramer and Darrow know it at every opportunity. But he couldn't faze them and they wouldn't relent. Convinced the girl had the book containing the incriminating evidence, they knew she had to be stopped before she could hand it over to the marshal in Blall City.

'There's nothing to say she would head for Blall City,' Conway had argued. 'Annie Burch is a smart woman, and she would know we would figure that is where she would go, so she might even make the run down to Salt Lake City.'

Momentarily, that had thrown the mine manager and the crooked sheriff, and their shock had shown on their faces. But Darrow, recovering quickly, had shaken his head.

'No. Weather is too bad for that, I figure. She knows she could get caught in a blizzard in that canyon country to the south. Lot of folk have died in there after getting lost. She would make for the nearest place she could turn the book over to the law and that is Blall City. We are

107

gonna stop her from getting there and you are helping us, Alonzo, so get used to the idea. Grab a gun and your coat 'cause we are movin' out pronto!'

So Alonzo Conway had gone along, hating every moment. He was a townsman: he didn't even like riding and he sure as hell had no love for mountains that from time to time were blotted out by fierce snowstorms.

As the posse of ten – Darrow, Kramer, Conway, Powell and the half dozen hard case miners – gathered round the ruins of the old way station in the crispness of the still morning, the saloon keeper was hoping the weather would hold. They could be in Blall City by sundown with a little luck and hard riding and he wouldn't mind making an extra effort, just to be sure he slept snug and comfortable tonight. In fact, a short sojourn in the County Seat seemed quite attractive to him now.

'Went into the timber, Mr Darrow,' Powell said, pointing to the obvious trail leading towards the trees. He was pathetically eager to atone for having allowed the lynch party to fail.

'Think we are blind, dummy?' growled Ocie Kramer. 'No place else they could have gone.' He looked at the miner who had been scouting around the area where the trio had spent the night. 'Any signs of a campfire, Isaac?'

The man shook his head. 'They must have rid out the cold.'

'Let's get into them trees and see what kind of trail they left. Isaac, take one man with you and ride around the timber up towards the rim. See if you can maybe spot where they came out. Could save us some time.'

The two miners started to ride off but not before Powell glared his hatred at Kramer as he set his mount in alongside Darrow's.

'Far side of that ridge is mighty bare, Mr Darrow. If they went up and over, they would have left plenty of tracks there. I could take a look and save us some time,' Powell suggested.

The mine manager nodded. 'Go ahead, Isaac. Ocie, send someone else other than Isaac for your search of the rim.'

Powell spurred away, eager to please and Kramer scowled after the big foreman. 'We wouldn't be here, if that fool hadn't fouled up the necktie party for the drifter.'

'No sense in that kind of talk, Ocie,' Gideon Darrow said. 'He is trying hard to make it up to us. Now let's move.'

They were surprised that they didn't find the three-some's tracks in the timber. And it seemed they had been obliterated when they had left the trees, too, for there were no telltale hoof prints on the far side of the ridge.

'Has to be that blasted drifter, Reason Conant,' Sheriff Kramer growled as they sat their mounts on the crest of the ridge, feeling the bite of the thinner air and the first probing fingers of a wind that could easily build up into another blizzard. 'Cooper McCarty didn't know that much about covering tracks. They had to have come this way though.'

'Unless they turned south towards Salt Lake City,' Conway said with considerable satisfaction, panting as he clung to his steaming mount. He pointed back along the ridge to the south where the bare rock face, too steep to hold the snow, glinted in the sun like metal. 'A horseman could ride along there, if he took it slow and steady.'

Darrow frowned. 'You're right, Alonzo, damned if you're not.' He swung back to the sheriff. 'What do you reckon, Ocie?'

'Still, don't think they would risk ridin' that far when blizzards could trap them – but there ain't no easy trail here that much is sure. This wind that's sprung up might have helped cover any tracks they left, but I doubt if it's been blowing long enough for that.'

'We better split up,' Darrow said suddenly. 'We can't take the chance that they didn't head south for Salt Lake City. Clay, take Mort and a couple of the others and get down south. Only go as far as Rondo Canyon. If you are sure you ain't passed them or picked up a track by that point, forget it. They would have to leave some sign in that distance. Isaac, maybe you better go with them.'

'Aw, I'd rather ride with your group, Mr Darrow, sir,' Powell said. 'I know these hills, but I dunno the south country as well as Clay. Lemme ride with you. I will show you I can do a good job. Gimme a chance to make up for that lynch mob thing, Mr Darrow.'

Kramer curled his lip but the mine manager nodded curtly. 'All right, Isaac. I forgot you used to live in these hills. You will be better with us. The rest of you get movin'. If you cut sign in the next hour, send a man back. Don't fire any shots. We don't want to warn them. Understood?'

'Sure thing, boss,' Clay said and, after picking his men, led the group away to the south.

Conway swore softly. 'Damn it, I thought we had them dead to rights, out here in the cold when we came over this ridge.'

Kramer grinned to him coldly. 'Don't go figuring on any soft beds for a spell just yet, Alonzo. This Conant's no

110

fool. We are gonna have us one helluva time runnin' him down. But we better do it, pronto. We don't even know how far ahead they are.'

'One thing is for sure,' Isaac Powell said slowly. 'If they come up this way, they ain't headed directly for Blall City, and that means we have got ourselves a real manhunt on our hands.'

His words did nothing to raise the morale of the hunters.

'We will find them,' gritted the sheriff. 'They can run around these hills until hell freezes over, but we will find them in the end and it's gonna be a real pleasure to put bullets in their heads.'

'Amen to that,' Gideon Darrow said tightly.

They knew it would be foolish to head directly into the part of the hills where the Youngs lived, so McCarty led them on a circuitous route, taking them through some deep canyons where the horses floundered to make headway through the snowdrifts.

There was no point in trying to cover their tracks, for the snow was powdery and fell back into the hoof prints. Any tracker worth their salt, of course, would soon discover the trail, but they didn't waste time trying to wipe them out completely.

In the two days they had been in the hills, they had only once caught sight of the posse. They had seen the slow-moving dots of a half dozen men on a distant range. They appeared to be searching for tracks. It was too far to make positive identifications, but they knew it was the posse and that Sheriff Kramer would be somewhere amongst them.

'Reckon it's time to start headin' for these friends of yours, Deputy,' Reason called as they rode out of a draw and were faced with timber-dotted slopes, leading to a snow-covered fold between the hills. The wind was howling, lifting a few swirls of snow, but there had been no blizzards since the first night. They didn't know how much longer the good weather would hold.

'Yeah, was thinkin' the same thing,' McCarty agreed. 'You OK, Annie?'

The girl, her face pinched with cold and fatigue, smiled faintly. 'Hungry, that's all.'

They grunted, for their grub was running low and they had been rationing it. Their bellies growled constantly, and the fact that they couldn't risk heating drinks or food added to their discomfort.

'All right. I figure if we make a fast run after sundown, I can get us there before the morning. But it means ridin' all night through high country and it's gonna be mighty cold. You two game?'

McCarty was pleased to be nominally in charge of the operation and it showed in his tone of voice and confident bearing. He looked challengingly at Conant as he spoke, but got no argument from the drifter. Reason was quite content to let the deputy take charge at this time.

So they rode through the night, pausing to cover some of their more obvious tracks. McCarty took two wrong turns up dead-end canyons, but just on sun up they topped a rise and the deputy's face suddenly brightened as he reined in and pointed down into a small valley. The trio saw a log cabin, with wood smoke already beginning to curl up from outbuildings with sod roofs, a corral and barn, some chickens and a sorry-looking vegetable patch.

There was a small, peaked structure of logs in the yard with steps leading down under it, which Reason figured to be a root cellar.

'That's the Youngs,' McCarty said, scrubbing a hand across his face, in an effort to bring himself more awake, for it had been a long, cold, tiring night on the trail. His nostrils twitched. 'Damn, I believe I can smell bacon fryin'!'

Reason's mouth watered. 'You got a better nose than me, then. But, for heaven's sake, the notion of bacon and eggs would be enough to make me ride down there, even if I knew Kramer was waiting with a loaded shotgun.'

'I-I think I would risk riding right along with you, Mr Conant,' Annie said. She looked very pale and weary and held tightly to the saddle horns.

'Well, let's go see what the Youngs are havin' for breakfast, huh?' suggested the young deputy, heeling his mount forward.

The Widow Young was younger than Reason had expected. He figured she was only in her early forties and Chet, the son, was about twenty-four. He figured Mrs Young must have married while still in her teens. She was a woman who had obviously experienced a lot of hardship, living as she did in such wild country, but she was a cheerful soul and made the fugitives feel welcome.

'Any friend of Cooper McCarty's is welcome to whatever is under my roof,' she told Reason Conant and the girl. 'Coop was good to me and my boy and I won't ever forget that.'

Narrow shouldered and lantern jawed, Chet Young was, nonetheless, a strong young man. Muscles ripped beneath his patched, homespun shirt, which he wore over red flannel underwear. He seemed impervious to the cold and didn't put on a coat to go outside unless his mother insisted. The same applied to boots. He padded around barefooted in the cabin and outside in the snow. He was taciturn and uneasy around strangers but was neverthe-less hospitable and couldn't do enough for Annie. He literally fell over his feet in his efforts to please her.

Reason noticed there was a Winchester .66 repeater hanging on nails above the fireplace, together with an old muzzle-loading Zouave, while the Winchester was mainly for 'protection'. By the looks of the coating of dust on the weapon, the drifter figured the cabin hadn't needed 'protecting' in a long, long time.

Over a hot breakfast of bacon, cornpone and coffee, Cooper McCarty told the Youngs of their predicament.

'We don't want to impose on you, Mrs Young,' Annie added quickly when the deputy had finished, 'or endan-ger you in any way. We just thought you might know of someplace where we could hide out for a few days, until the sheriff and his crooked posse get tired of searching for us.'

The widow sniffed and, to Reason's surprise, took a charred old corncob pipe from her apron's pocket and leaned towards the fireplace. She picked up a glowing twig, lit the pipe, then puffed pungent tobacco smoke into the air.

'Well, that ain't too difficult, I guess. Plenty of caves hereabouts, or out yonder in the canyon country,' she said easily.

'I got a better idea than the caves, Ma,' Chet said slowly and flushed uncomfortably when they all looked at him. He fidgeted with a loose thread on his frayed coveralls.

114

'There's an old trapper's cabin out on Drawknife Ridge. From the outside it looks to be in ruins, but inside there's two rooms still roofed over, and if the weight of the snow hasn't caved 'em in, it'd be a real good place to hide out.' He looked towards the deputy. 'Bein' on the ridge, you'll have a good view most of the way around too. And there's a spring nearby that might be froze over now, but if you dig down a ways it'll flow again. Real sweet water, too. Logs might need some choppin', but if you wasn't gonna be there that long, you could just stuff some in gunnysacks. We got plenty in the root cellar.'

'That sounds perfect,' Reason opined. 'But who knows about it, Chet?'

'Only me and Ma. Pa showed it to us once. It was being used by a bunch of outlaws. They wasn't real bad men, and he was helpin' 'em a little, I guess. The cabin goes back a long ways and whoever built it is long dead, or plumb forgot all about it.'

'Seems ideal,' Cooper McCarty allowed, turning to the widow. 'Could we get some grub off you, Mrs Young? We're mighty low and …'

'I'll rustle you up somethin', flour and coffee and so on. But you might have to be careful with a campfire. Bein' on the ridge, the smoke would be seen a long ways away.'

'Providing someone was lookin' for it, Ma,' Chet Young said.

'They won't give up easy,' Reason pointed out. 'We're hoping to throw 'em by holing up for a few days, but they have got a lot to lose and they might just keep on looking. Which means they will maybe be around to you folk sometime.'

The woman clamped her teeth on the stem of the pipe. 'They'll get nothin' out of us! Don't you worry about that, we owe too much to Coop to be helpin' his enemies find him.' She spat into the fireplace. 'Chet, you go git some vittles outa the root cellar for Coop and his friends. And put your jacket and boots on, you hear?'

Chet flushed deeply. He murmured, 'Yes, Ma,' and looked towards Annie. She gave him a warm smile and his ears turned purple with embarrassment.

Reason stood by the one glazed window in the cabin, stooping a little and watching the hills. He had an uneasy feeling that they hadn't shaken the posse yet.

Cooper McCarty's kin in the hills were named Trundell, being related on his mother's side. They were farmers and also ran a few sheep, so they were not very popular in a community that was predominantly cattle-minded. As a consequence, the Trundells patronized the stores of Blall City more often than those in Biggs, but they still ran into trouble fairly frequently.

Despite what anyone said, a sheep man did smell different to a cattleman and the fact sparked many a brawl in the saloons of both towns. So the Trundells developed a thick-skinned attitude and learned to use their fists and guns well, knowing they had to, in order to hold their own against the cattlemen.

Kramer and Darrow knew they were a tough bunch, so they spread out their meagre forces when they came to the valley where the Trundells ran their spread. Alonzo Conway, gun in hand, shook his head slowly.

'Still reckon we are wasting our time,' he said. 'Cooper McCarty wouldn't come here for help. Too obvious.'

'And he might think that's exactly what we would think, so he had go to the Trundells,' growled Darrow.

'You're guessing,' Conway said, angry because he was still out in the wilderness. 'Guessing wild.'

'What the hell else have we got to go on?' snapped Sheriff Ocie Kramer, checking his rifle. 'We have seen no worthwhile tracks, and had no word from Clay and the others. They didn't just sprout wings and fly away. We gotta look at all the possibilities. And now I'm gettin' mighty tired of ridin' all over the State of Utah lookin' for them three.'

'I'm in agreement with you on that score, leastways,' murmured Conway.

'Well, we know they ain't yet turned up in Blall City, or Reid Sloat would have gotten word to us,' Darrow said. 'Like Ocie says, Alonzo, we got no choice but to move in on the Trundells. And, listen, you men, they are gonna fight hard, but we don't want 'em all dead. Someone's gotta be left alive long enough to tell us what we want to know. Savvy?'

The men nodded and moved to their positions. Then, just as they were about to launch the attack on the group of cabins below in the valley, there came a ragged volley of rifle fire from the trees around them.

One of the miners threw up his hands and fell face down in the snow. He lay unmoving, a spreading stain at one side of his head. A second man, standing beside big Isaac Powell, spun off balance and sat down with a grunt of pain, staring in disbelief at his left shoulder, where a huge chunk of clothing and flesh had been torn away. Then he paled as blood spurted and, howling in agony, he rolled over and crawled away on all fours. Guns hammered again and the crawling man shuddered, fell onto his side and kicked out the last moments of his life.

'The goddamn Trundells!' yelled Kramer, who was still mounted.

He hipped in the saddle and fired his rifle into the trees, working lever and trigger, rattling out a fast volley. Bark and snow flew and a man in a sheepskin jacket stumbled out from behind a tree, dropping a smoking rifle. Kramer swore at the man, levered in another shell, beaded swiftly and blew a hole in his head.

Three other Trundells quit the timber fast and ran back towards the rim, where they were given covering fire by their kin, who were already staked out up there. But Gideon Darrow, Conway and Powell were now mounted and they set their horses after the running men, weaving back and forth in an effort to dodge the lead hammering down from the rim. One of the running Trundells went down and before he could get to his feet, Kramer rode his horse over him and, for good measure, fired point blank into his back. Then he wrenched at the reins, swerving his horse to one side and hitting the slope at a run. He would have made it right to the rim except for a deep drift that trapped his horse. Kramer knew he would be a sitting duck if he didn't move, so within seconds of the animal sinking up to its belly, he threw himself from the saddle, hearing bullets zipping into the snow about him. He rolled and somersaulted away from the whickering, plunging horse and just as he reached the cover of a deadfall, the animal died with a bullet through its head. Kramer swore, his rifle seeking the gunmen lining the rim.

Darrow's gun cut down another of the fleeing Trundells, but the third man made it, although he was dragging his left leg as he dropped from sight. A heavy volley came from the rim, then there was a sudden silence as the posse men scattered for cover.

'Get on up there!' yelled Kramer, floundering through the snow towards a horse that had belonged to one of the dead miners. 'They're on the run! I heard a horse whinny!'

Powell went forward without hesitation, lashing his mount up the slope, but Darrow and Conway held back. The big man topped the ridge, reined in, threw his rifle to his shoulder and began shooting.

By the time the others had joined him – Kramer now mounted on the dead miner's horse – the Trundells were riding into the cluster of cabins on the valley floor. There were three of them, including the man with the wounded leg, who was riding double with another man.

'Let's get down there, before they got time to settle in!' snapped Kramer and spurred his mount forward.

The others hesitated, but only momentarily. Then they swept down the slope and into the valley so speedily that the Trundells were still helping the wounded man into the nearest hut when they rode into the yard.

Guns blasted from one of the other cabins and Powell, looking that way, said, 'Womenfolk!'

'They're Trundells,' replied Gideon Darrow. 'They want to fight us, they can take their chances, same as the men.'

Lead was raking the yard as they ran for cover behind the barn. When they dismounted, panting, Conway said, 'Listen, instead of dodging lead out here, why don't we burn the varmints out? Them cabins are close together. Set one afire and it would soon spread.'

'How do we set it afire?' snapped Kramer. 'You want to run up there and touch it off with a match?'

Conway flushed and said nothing, but he was looking at Isaac Powell.

The big ramrod glanced at Darrow. 'You want them cabins burned, Mr Darrow?'

The mine manager pursed his lips. 'It would sure bring them out into the open, Isaac.'

Powell nodded and began testing the planks in the wall of the barn. He found two that were loose and ripped them out. Lead splintered the corner of the barn as guns in both cabins opened up. Isaac Powell ignored the bullets and stepped into the barn's gloom. The others heard the hollow sounds of drums being moved about and a few minutes later, Powell appeared, grinning.

'Buckboard in there, Mr Darrow. I've loaded it with hay and found me a drum of coal oil. I can set it alight and push it clear up against the nearest cabin.'

'Do that, Isaac. And keep your head down.'

'Don't worry none about me, Mr Darrow. I will do this chore right, you'll see.'

Powell went back inside the barn and kicked the big doors open, leaping back as guns from the closest cabin raked the area. Then, with the piled hay for cover, he lifted the shaft and manoeuvred the heavy buckboard into line with the doorway. A few minutes later a match flared and there was a roar as the oil-soaked hay burst into flames.

Pieces of the blazing hay spilled to the ground as the guns in the cabins were turned onto the buckboard and bullets tore through its burning load. Powell dug in with his boots, slipped a couple of times, then, his ugly face empurpled with the effort, moved the heavy vehicle forward, actually managing to increase his pace to a run before releasing the shaft and throwing himself behind a heavy-sided water trough. The trough caved in as a shotgun thundered and water erupted like a geyser, but Powell rolled under the trough and escaped injury.

The buckboard's wheels slammed into the stoop of the nearest cabin. The vehicle jolted as it came to an abrupt standstill and the blazing hay spilled forward and piled itself against the cabin door. The weathered wood caught almost instantly and the whole cabin front was ablaze in minutes. Behind the wall of flame someone screamed, then the door of the far cabin opened and two women emerged clutching rifles, shooting at the intruders as they ran to help their kinfolk in the burning cabin.

Darrow's face was impassive as he beaded the first woman and put a bullet through her chest. Her body was flung backwards by the impact and landed in an untidy heap. The second woman screamed and, throwing her gun aside, sought a way into the burning cabin. Ocie Kramer settled himself at the barn corner and picked her off with a single shot. She fell to her knees in the snow, teetered for a moment then toppled sideways.

By then, the heat inside the cabin must have been unbearable and two men suddenly burst through the flames, one supporting the other, who was dragging his leg. Powell's gun blasted and the unwounded man jerked, released his hold on the other and fell, floundering, in the snow. Isaac Powell finished him with two more well-placed shots and the man with the wounded leg dragged himself further away from the fire. Powell was drawing a bead on him when he remembered Darrow's warning that they wanted someone alive and held his fire.

The remaining man in the cabin was still screaming, then he suddenly staggered out, ablaze head to foot. Darrow, Powell and Kramer merely stood watching the man's agony as he fell to the snow and rolled around trying to extinguish the flames that seared him. But Alonzo Conway, feeling his stomach heave, drew a bead with shaking hands and shot the man. It took three bullets to end the man's agony and the others stared at Conway, silently censuring him for spoiling their 'fun'. Conway moved away and noisily threw up behind the barn.

'This man's still alive, Mr Darrow,' called Isaac Powell as he stood over the man with the wounded leg. 'He's burned up some, but he's still drawing a breath.'

'Yeah, well looks like he's the only one who is,' Kramer said, straightening from where he had been examining one of the women. 'Both women are dead and so is this other poor bastard.'

Darrow was beside Powell now. He nudged the wounded man roughly with his boot toe. 'We are looking for your kin, Cooper McCarty. Seen him lately?'

The man, skin burned from his face, hair singed off one side of his head, stared incredulously up at the big miner. 'Cooper? Th-that's what this is all about?' He shook his head slowly, gasping and grimacing in pain. 'We seen you moving in – figured you was cowmen. We-we ain't seen Cooper in a coon's age.'

Powell kicked the man brutally and screwed his fingers into his singed hair, but Darrow signalled for him to hold off. He knelt and looked into Trundell's pain-filled eyes.

'Sorry, feller, this is too important for us to just take your word. Have to let Isaac here work on you some, so that when you answer our questions we will know you're speaking gospel – or Isaac will be waiting to start all over again.'

'No! We ain't seen Cooper! Wh-what's he done anyways?'

Darrow jerked his head at Powell. The big ramrod stooped and dragged the wounded man to his feet. He screamed in pain and fainted. Powell lifted him effortlessly under one arm and carried him around behind the burning building.

Darrow and Kramer smoked quietly as the cabin gradually burned away to charred framework and Trundell screamed as Powell worked on him. Alonzo Conway stood back, pale and sick-looking.

'Is this really necessary, for Christ's sake?' he asked hoarsely. 'You can see McCarty ain't here.'

'Might have been here, you fool,' snapped Kramer. 'We gotta know. If he ain't showed, maybe this feller, his kin, will know where he might go. The girl don't know anyone she can ask for help, nor does the drifter, Conant. We got to work around Cooper McCarty. Ah, here's Powell now. Well, dummy? What did he have to say?'

The big foreman wiped his hands on his jacket and glared coldly at the sheriff before shifting his gaze to Darrow.

'Cooper ain't been here, Mr Darrow. I would bet on that. I made him tell me if the deputy had any other friends here, but all he would say was somethin' about Widow's Gap. Guess he meant all McCarty's friends are there.'

Darrow grunted. 'Well, we know that much.' He frowned and looked at Kramer. 'They wouldn't have been smart enough to have doubled back to town, would they?'

'To Widow's Gap? Hell, no, Gideon. What would they gain? They would still have to get the book to the marshal at Blall City.'

'Yeah,' Darrow agreed reluctantly. He sighed. 'Well, we played a hunch and it didn't come off. Looks like we better get back to the hills.'

'We are wastin' time,' Conway complained. 'Why don't we just ride on to Blall City and wait for them to show up?'

'Art's already there,' said Darrow, sounding annoyed. 'We want them stopped dead, long before they get anywhere near Blall City. It will be a damn sight harder to nail them once they get to the marshal, so talk sense, Alonzo.' He turned to Powell. 'Isaac, you clean up here; dump the bodies someplace. We will get into the hills and look for tracks. Meet us – uh – say at Shadow Peak. You ought to be there by sundown. If you can't make it by then, don't try to climb that peak in the dark. Wait someplace till daylight. Understand?'

Powell's face clouded, but he nodded, knowing he had landed this dirty chore as part of his 'punishment' for not pulling off the lynch party as planned. If Trundell had provided some helpful information, it would have put Powell back in Darrow's good books and that was mighty important to the big foreman.

He worked hard at digging a common grave for the dead Trundells and, being a thorough man, he even went up to the ridge, brought down the bodies and dumped them into the hole. He had left the man he had tortured till last for he was not quite dead. He hung suspended between life and death, bloody and only semi-conscious.

Isaac Powell knelt beside the man and slapped his face brutally to arouse him from the coma-like state. Trundell screamed thinly, eyes flying wide to stare in abject fear at Powell.

'You could have gotten me off the hook with my boss, mister, but you didn't. You ain't much alive, but you got enough left in you to tell me one more time: where would Cooper McCarty be likely to go for help?'

The man's slack, blood flecked lips moved and he made guttural sounds deep in his throat as he tried to speak. He vaguely saw Powell's hands move and screamed in anticipation of more pain. Sobbing, he managed a few words.

'T-told you. Wid-Widow's ...'

Powell cuffed him savagely. 'Goddamn it, he wouldn't have gone back to Widow's Gap! Mr Darrow already said that!'

The man shook his head feebly. 'N-not G-Gap. Y-Young. Coop h-helped her ...'

His voice trailed away and Powell shook him and used every trick he knew to bring the man around, but he was unsuccessful.

The man was dead.

'By God!' he breathed. 'Widow Young! Wait until Mr Darrow finds out about this! I'll be on his good side again.'

Suddenly a cunning grin twisted his scarred mouth. Certainly taking this information to Darrow would help make up for fouling up the lynch party, but if he could bring the bodies of McCarty, Conant and the girl, with the book ... He felt dizzy just thinking about it and, having made the decision, he hurriedly mounted and rode off into the sundown.

If he pulled this off – and he aimed to – he would be in Gideon Darrow's good books for the rest of this life.

CHAPTER 14

Widow Kay Young packed one more layer of food into the sack before pushing it across the table towards Chet, who was jamming his old felt hat onto the back of his head.

'You put on your jacket and shoes, mind, before you quit this here cabin, you hear me, boy?' she told him, as she reached for her corncob pipe and lit it up again. 'Gets mighty cold in them hills, as you well know, and that snow ain't gonna hold off much longer.'

'Aw, all right, Ma, geez, quit yer fussin' over me,' Chet said, surly, and donned his sheepskin jacket.

Widow Young jammed her pipe into one corner of her mouth, and puffing away, fastened the front of the jacket with the rawhide ties. Chet suffered her to do this, although he could not understand why he could never get her to understand that he simply wasn't bothered by the cold.

He slipped on his boots, but had to sit down and take them off again when his mother handed him a pair of woollen socks she had knitted and told him to put them on. Finally, he met with her approval and she handed him the grub sack.

'Now you tell Coop and his friends that we've heard there are men riding through the hills asking after 'em, so they had best not use a fire any more than necessary, you hear me? That sack's full of good, home-cooked grub and it will be better for 'em than hardtack. They can eat it cold, but at least it'll taste right. You got it, boy?'

Chet rolled his eyes, then quickly hoped his mother had not noticed it. 'Yeah, Ma, I got it, quit yer fussin'.'

'All right, then you get goin' and come back here as soon as you can. That ole cow in the barn's about to drop her calf any time now and I'm gonna need help with that,' Ma Young reminded her son.

'I'll be as quick as I can, Ma,' Chet said.

Chet dutifully kissed the weathered cheek she lifted towards him, picked up the grub sack and sauntered out to the yard where his horse stood, saddled and ready to go. He rode out swiftly, pausing three times, as usual, to wave farewell to his mother. It was a ritual they went through every time he left the house.

To be honest, Chet wasn't sure if it was more for his mother's benefit, or his.

He urged the horse into a fast lope but once he had crossed the rise, slowed down long enough to undo the ties of his heavy jacket. He would have liked to have kicked off his boots, too, but he couldn't tie neat bows in the laces the way Ma could and she would have realized he had taken them off. He could easily explain why the jacket was undone, by saying he had taken it off in the trapper's cabin where Cooper and the other two visitors were holed up.

His mind preoccupied, Chet Young rode on through the hills, unaware that big Isaac Powell was following his progress from a nearby ridge, keeping his mount in what-ever cover was offered so that he wasn't seen.

By the time Chet Young came within sight of the old trapper's cabin hidden deep in the hills, Isaac Powell was only a mile behind him and following the trail Chet had left with almost no effort on his part.

Dismounting in a clump of trees just below the crest of a ridge, Powell grinned crookedly to himself as he slid his rifle out of the saddle scabbard and levered a shell into the breech. He leaned against a tree trunk, looking out covertly, watching Chet Young being greeted by Cooper McCarty at the cabin. The deputy held a rifle as he leaned in the doorway, talking with the youth who was handing him a gunnysack that looked to be stuffed with food. Powell's empty belly growled for he had not eaten for many hours, but he tried to ignore the pangs of hunger, as he strained to see into the gloom of the cabin. The roof had caved in in a couple of places and the windows were like vacant eyes, covered only by tattered blankets draped across the openings. The door, too, looked a mite rickety and all in all, he was surprised the old cabin was still standing. He hadn't known it existed, although he knew the whole area was dotted with aban-doned trappers' cabins.

Someone came into the doorway behind the deputy and Powell's pulse quickened when he recognized Annie Burch. Hell, he thought, with her in the cabin, the odds were the drifter was there as well. Likely, he was keeping well out of sight until the caller had been identified.

As Chet Young followed the deputy inside and closed the door, Powell could hardly contain his excitement. If he had all three trapped in that cabin, it would be like shooting fish in a barrel. He would kill them and deliver their carcasses to Mr Darrow ... after, of course, making the girl tell him where the book was. His excitement increased at the thought of working on the girl.

Crouching low, he dodged from tree to tree, working his way down the slope, pausing at the edge of the clump to look at the cabin. Nothing was stirring, so he made a fast run for a nest of boulders jutting out of the snow. Panting, he flattened himself against one of the boulders and ran his tongue over his lips. Another hundred yards or so and he would be at the cabin. Once there, he would burst through that rickety door and start blasting at anything that moved. Too bad he didn't have a shotgun, but he could work a repeating rifle mighty fast and he would just keep firing until he had downed them all.

'Don't move, Powell!'

The big foreman stiffened, almost jumping off the ground at the sound of the voice right behind him and the nudging of a gun barrel being pressed against his spine. He swallowed audibly.

'Just ease down the hammer on that rifle and place it on the ground there. Try anything else or try to be smart and I'll blow that ugly head of yours clean off!'

Powell had never heard Reason Conant speak, so he did not recognize the voice. But he knew it was not Cooper McCarty or Chet Young and it sure wasn't the girl, so it had to be the drifter. The big puzzle was, how the hell had the man got out here and got the jump on him?

'Move it!' snapped Conant, increasing the pressure of the gun muzzle to the man's spine.

'Where the hell did you come from?' Isaac Powell

wanted to know as he eased down the rifle's hammer and reached out towards the flat patch of ground the drifter had indicated.

'Been watching you for a spell,' Reason told him, eyeing the big miner's every movement warily. 'Had some traps set and was out checkin' 'em. If you had taken time to look, you might have seen my tracks leading away from the rear of the cabin. But guess you only had eyes for Chet Young and Cooper down at the cabin.'

'Spotted the girl, so I thought you was inside too,' Powell said in a strained voice as he slid the rifle on the ground – there was still a covering of snow, but it only helped to slide the weapon.

'Where's the sheriff and the others?' Reason prodded.

'Oh, they're around,' Powell said, then cursed as he over-balanced and sprawled on his hands and knees in the snow.

Reason wasn't surprised, for the ground was a tad wet and slippery and required the big foreman to bend far out to reach the area Reason had indicated to place the rifle. But suddenly, Powell whirled, his huge shovel-sized hand scooping up snow and grit from the ground. The slush was suddenly flying towards Reason's face and he cursed and leapt aside, but didn't squeeze the trigger. He did not know how close the rest of the posse might be and he did not want to risk them hearing the gunshot and come riding in.

Powell's attack came hard on the heels of the slush. Reason managed to kick him in the midriff, but the man was heavily padded by his fur jacket and did little more than grunt in response to the kick. Powell swung his fist around in a wide arc, Reason caught the blow on the

131

top of his right shoulder and was sent sprawling. Then a massive boot slammed down on his wrist and ground his gun hand deep into the snow and down to the hard earth beneath. He released the gun and sobbed in pain as Powell triumphantly knocked the hat from his head and twisted his fingers in his hair. Laughing, Powell pulled Reason upright with the drifter frantically clawing at his big hand. Reason's feet actually left the ground and he kicked wildly as Powell flung him against a rock, which he hit with such force the breath was driven from him.

Reason toppled forward and Powell kneed him in the face, forcing him back across the rock. Then the big man aimed a kick at the drifter's groin. Reason twisted aside desperately, Powell's kick missed and he yelled as the toe of his boot crashed into a boulder, almost breaking his ankle. He hopped around, grasping his injured foot, and Reason seized the opportunity to launch himself bodily at the man. He rammed his shoulder into Powell's back and knocked him face-first into the boulder. Then Reason, locking his hands together, clubbed Isaac Powell on the back of the skull, smashing his face down on the rock again.

Powell screamed and reared back, hands covering his face, blood oozing between his splayed fingers. Then with one hand still covering his face, he clawed for his six-gun.

Reason had no choice now; he had to shoot and the only gun in sight was Powell's rifle – his own Colt being buried somewhere in the snow nearby. He lunged for the weapon, scooped up the Winchester, snapped the hammer back and twisting frantically in mid-air, squeezed the trigger. Powell staggered under the impact of the bullet, but his Colt thundered and lead whined off the flat rock as Reason Conant, scrambling up onto his knees, levered and triggered three times. The shots came so close together they sounded like one prolonged roar.

Isaac Powell's head snapped back and his huge legs buckled as a bullet took him through the middle of the face. He was actually dead then, but the other two slugs tore into him, one ripping through his neck, the third slamming into his big heart. Snow erupted as his huge body crashed forward, boots kicking spasmodically.

Reason was sitting on a flat rock, nursing his own wounds when Cooper McCarty, Chet Young and Annie Burch came panting up to stare at the dead miner. The drifter lifted his head slowly.

'Dunno how far away the posse is, but I reckon that shootin' will likely be bringing them our way, shortly.'

The girl paled and looked swiftly towards the deputy.

Cooper was glaring at Chet Young. 'Hell, that means we will have to hit the trail again,' he said. 'He must have followed you here, Chet. Didn't you check, boy?'

Chet shuffled his feet and flushed uncomfortably. 'I-I thought I had.'

McCarty sighed. 'Well, there's nothing to be done about it now. We had best move on down and start packing up.'

Annie helped Reason to his feet and he trudged through the snow beside her, aching from the exertion of the fight with the massive mining foreman.

The fugitives' fears that Sheriff Kramer and the others might have heard the gunfire were well-founded.

Because the wind had dropped again and the strange

stillness that often comes after a snowstorm had settled over the hills, the noise from the guns crackled crisply through the mountain air and carried for miles – all the way to Shadow Peak.

The sheriff immediately identified the sound as that of gunfire.

'Gunfire?' echoed Alonzo Conway irritably, wanting only to get back to the comforts of his saloon. He did not feel safe out in the hills or on a horse. 'You're plumb loco. No gun I ever heard made a sound like that.'

'That's 'cause you live in a fog of cigarette smoke between four walls, Alonzo,' the sheriff told him. 'I'm tellin' you that was gunfire we just heard.'

'Any idea where it came from?' Gideon Darrow asked, prepared to believe the sheriff without question on this subject.

Ocie Kramer shook his head slowly. 'Just a guess, but I would say somewhere in that direction.' He chopped a hand towards the northeast.

'What do you think it was? I mean, a shootout or someone hunting?' Conway asked, trying to hide his nervousness.

'Hard to say. I ain't certain but I reckon there was at least two guns,' the sheriff answered.

'Well, whatever it was, it was a long ways off,' growled Conway. 'And it's getting dark. We gonna stay here for the night or what? It don't look like Powell's going to show.'

Kramer and Darrow held a quick conference and decided to investigate the shooting.

'But it'll be dark in less than an hour!' protested the saloon keeper.

'It'll be a full moon tonight,' Kramer said, pointing to

the silver sphere already beginning to glow in the eastern sky. 'No wind. Whoever fired those shots would have left tracks and we'll see them plain in the moonlight.'

Conway swore. 'You're guessin' that gunfire – if it was gunfire and I still ain't convinced it was – was somethin' to do with the deputy, the girl and the drifter.'

'Well, we know they're in the hills someplace and Blall City lies to the northeast. They've got to eat so they might have been hunting,' Kramer pointed out. 'And if they weren't they were tradin' lead with someone. Could have been Isaac. He should have finished that chore at the Trundells' long since. Maybe he cut their trail and tried to take 'em alone – he's a mite loco, that way. We can't just pass it up, Alonzo.'

Conway tightened his lips. He knew they were right but, goddamn it, it meant more time spent out here in the freezing cold where the air cut into a man's lungs like a knife. It was just almighty damn irritating and that was certain. Alonzo Conway was miserable and wasn't hiding the fact.

'I hope to hell we ain't gonna be ridin' all over the hills on some wild goose chase,' he complained, determined to have the last word as they moved off.

It almost was a wild goose chase, for the intervening hills between Shadow Peak and the trapper's cabin had distorted the sound of the gunshots. Kramer's guess that the sound had come from the northeast had been a good one, but that took in a lot of country and by midnight, they were mighty cold. When they found a rock overhang, screened at one end by thick brush, Kramer gave in to Conway's constant pleading to stop and bed down for the night.

The sheriff, convinced they were close to the three fugitives, had them on the trail before daylight. He made a lucky decision when he chose to lead them across a gulch and up a slope to a hogback ridge. It was a hard climb, and reaching the crest, they paused and looked down at the snow glistening in the early morning sun. Clearly visible below was a line of hoof prints.

Upon riding down to check the tracks, they found there were two sets. One rider had been trailing another.

'Looks as though you were right, Kramer,' Darrow said with some delight. 'Powell must have finished at the Trundells', spotted somebody and trailed after them.'

'Yeah, well, let's get moving ...'

The tracks led them into a hidden valley and there they found the body of Isaac Powell sprawled in the blood-stained snow. Although they figured the cabin would be empty, they approached it carefully anyways and went inside with drawn guns.

'They must have spotted Isaac and gunned him down, then hightailed it out of here,' said Darrow tautly.

'At least we know we are in the right area,' Kramer said. 'They're still headed for Blall City. Must have been goin' to lay low for a while, until they figured it was safe to make a run for it.'

'Do we head straight for Blall City, then?' asked Conway, eagerness in his voice.

'We scout for tracks, that's what we do,' snapped Kramer and went out of the cabin's rear door.

It took time but they eventually found hastily covered tracks. They were somewhat puzzled that four riders had ridden away from the cabin.

'The other rider could have been the one Powell

was followin'!' Darrow said, after giving it some serious thought. 'Must have been someone helpin' them.'

'Hell, does that mean we are up against an extra gun now?' the saloon keeper asked.

Kramer scratched at his stubble. 'Don't rightly know. Wouldn't be surprised if they split up somewhere either. What we gotta do is try to work out which way the gal goes. She's the one with the damn book.'

'Yes, that blasted book that just may be the death of us all,' murmured Conway.

But, by midday, they were still advancing very slowly, finding only a little sign here and there – and they were unable to tell whether the group had split up or not.

The hunters weren't happy with this; they had no choice but to push on. Then, mid-afternoon, they spotted movement on a ridge, a brief dark rippling against the glare of the sun, and Darrow took out his field glasses and swiftly focused them.

'It's them!' he exclaimed. 'By hell it is! The gal and – yeah that's your deputy, Ocie. His horse is looking lame, which is likely what is slowing them down. The drifter, Conant, is bringing up the rear.'

'What about the fourth rider?' asked the lawman, excitedly.

'Nope. Just the three is all I see. But they are the three we want. If someone was helping them, he likely veered off and went back home,' Darrow said coldly.

Ocie Kramer frowned thoughtfully. 'Could be,' he said cautiously. 'But I would like to know who it was and just where they are now.'

'To hell with them!' Darrow snapped, ramming the glasses back into his saddlebag. 'They're dropping out of sight beyond that ridge. Let's get after them! We can be right behind them before dark!'

CHAPTER 15

When the three fugitives had reached a timbered ridge soon after leaving the cabin, Chet Young announced that he was riding back to his mother. There was no reason, of course, for him to continue right on to Blall City with the others.

'Just keep under cover as much as you can, Chet,' Reason Conant told the young man. 'Try not to be seen and if you spot the sheriff and his posse, go to ground until they are out of sight.'

'I understand, Mr Conant,' Chet said with a nod. 'And I'm-I'm mighty sorry I led that big, ugly feller, Powell, to your cabin.'

'Don't worry about it, Chet, it has been taken care of,' the drifter said simply without any hit of emotion. 'Adios and thank your mother for all she has done for us. She is a fine woman.'

After Chet Young had left them, they continued riding through the moonlight, McCarty leading the way. Their progress was slow because of the time it took covering their tracks. They debated splitting up, but decided there was little to be gained by such a move. Reason believed that in truth the deputy did not want to let him out of his sight.

Continually plunging through the snowdrifts was mighty tiring for the horses, so they camped amongst some heavy timber, and built a small fire to brew coffee, sheltering it with rocks and screening it with branches. As soon as the coffee was made and the beans heated, they reluctantly dumped snow over the fire to douse it. Its warmth had been most welcome and the hot food, the first in days, was equally welcome to their stomachs.

They slept well. So well, in fact, that the sun was shining brightly when they woke.

'Hell, we have lost some time!' opined McCarty as he saddled his mount.

'Hour or so, it would appear,' Reason admitted. 'But I guess we needed the rest.' He turned to the girl. 'How long now before we sight Blall City?'

Annie, hastily tightening her mount's cinch strap, paused to look at the big drifter, who was already mounted.

'If we don't worry too much about covering our tracks, we could make it by sundown, going by the direct route, but I'm not sure that would be the wisest choice.'

'Hell, no,' said Reason. 'You can bet they will have someone watching the regular trails. Which way do you reckon, Deputy?'

Cooper McCarty straightened, placed his foot in the stirrup and nodded in the direction of the spine of the mountain range, where it snaked away into the blue haze.

'We ride along the divide, I reckon until we are directly above the town. Then we just go straight on down and come in from the rear,' he said with confidence.

140

'Sounds like a good plan,' Reason allowed. 'How long do you think it will take?'

'Well, I reckon we will lose half a day coverin' the extra distance and countin' the time it will take to cover our trail. With luck, I would say we ought to ride into Blall City by noon tomorrow,' McCarty replied.

'All right. That's our target then: Blall City by noon tomorrow. Barring accidents and blizzards and Kramer we ought to make it.' He winked at Annie to show her he was talking lightly but, although she gave him a faint smile, he saw she was worried.

They set off in single file with Cooper McCarty leading, the girl in the middle, and Reason Conant bringing up the rear. Both men held rifles in their gloved hands.

They kept constant watch, but did not see any sign of pursuit during the morning. It was not possible to keep off the skyline at all times. The very nature of the rugged country dictated whether they rode high on the ridge or just below. Where possible, they tried to ride with the ridge between them and the old trapper's cabin, out of view of their pursuers. But there were places this was not possible.

In the early afternoon, they ran into trouble, something all too familiar to Reason. And it looked mighty serious.

Cooper McCarty, riding in the lead, suddenly disappeared from sight with a wild yell, as his horse stepped into an incredibly deep snowdrift. Annie cried out in alarm and reined in her horse, wide-eyed. Reason spurred up beside her and grabbed her horse's reins, yanking her mount up onto the cap rock of the ridge.

She was skylined, but it could not be helped.

'Stay right there and don't move,' Reason snapped, quitting leather, and unslinging his rope. 'Deputy! You hear me?'

There was no immediate answer and Reason shook out the noose in his rope as he warily approached the caved-in depression in the snow, looked down, and was surprised to see only a blanket of snow in the bottom.

Suddenly, the snow erupted and Cooper McCarty's head appeared. Then his horse exploded up through the snow that had avalanched down on top of them when they had plunged into the unseen depression.

Reason tossed the rope down and McCarty snatched at it and swiftly got the loop under his arms. Reason dug in his boot heels so he wouldn't slip and heaved, slowly pulling the deputy onto firm ground. It was not easy; the loose snow kept falling down but finally McCarty, shivering and cursing, floundered out onto solid ground.

It was more difficult to free the horse. They had only one rope and the panic-stricken animal was making its situation worse by continually plunging and fighting the rope, which brought down more snow.

Using the girl's and Reason's horses and with Cooper braced on the cap rock and pulling, too, they slowly got the horse high enough for its hooves to find more solid footing. Eventually it was safely on the cap rock. It stood there, shaking itself, wild eyed and quivering.

Worse still, it had injured its foreleg.

'Gonna slow us down quite a bit,' Cooper McCarty said grimly, examining the animal's right foreleg. 'Tendon's pulled or twisted I would guess. It is already swelling …'

'Too dangerous to ride double yet,' Reason told him.

He gestured to the drift. 'If your mount had been carrying double, somebody could have been killed.'

'Sure,' agreed McCarty. 'I will ride him a spell longer, till the leg gives out altogether. But we are going to be behind schedule.'

'As long as we are moving,' Reason said, and they got underway again within minutes. But it was obvious that McCarty's mount was not going to go the distance.

The deputy continued to lead, not that he knew the way any better – for anyone but a blind man could follow the spine of the divide – but simply to set the pace for the others. They had to slow their mounts to match the speed of McCarty's horse.

That was how they came to be spotted by Gideon Darrow and the others, who were climbing the ridge in the early afternoon.

Reason Conant glanced at the deputy up ahead, and saw that the horse could not possibly carry him for much longer. It was limping so badly that Cooper McCarty had to actually cling to the saddle horn to keep from being thrown over the animal's head. The deep snow did not make the going any easier, although it helped cover their tracks for it tended to slide back and fill the hoof prints.

The drifter hipped in the saddle, and glanced back along the ridge to see if the trail was adequately covered.

It was then that he spotted the three pursuers far below, riding hell for leather, which meant they had already seen the fugitives.

'Sheriff Kramer!' Reason yelled and Annie jumped with shock and jerked her head around, alarm showing on her pale face. Reason pointed down, but she and the young deputy had already seen the pursuers.

'No point in keeping to the ridge now,' Cooper called back, lifting the reins. 'We better ride down and make for the regular trail. The sooner we get within spitting distance of Blall City now the better.'

'Hold up, Deputy!' Reason yelled, knowing the ride down the slope would throw even more strain on the injured horse, but Cooper McCarty was already riding over the far side of the ridge.

The animal whinnied in pain as it floundered down the ridge and Annie Burch screamed as it lost its footing on the steep snow slope and went down nose first, its neck twisting at such an angle that Reason knew it was broken – McCarty was flung violently over its head.

Reason moved his horse alongside the girl's and took hold of her mount's reins, steadying the animal. At the same time he watched as the deputy went sailing through the air. He hit the slope at such an angle that, instead of ploughing into the snow, he skidded along the hard surface and crashed into an outcrop of rocks.

Annie's hands covered her mouth as the deputy's slide was brought to an abrupt halt and he lay against the rocks, unmoving.

'Follow me, but sit well back on your mount's rump and don't let him start to plunge!' snapped Reason, sliding off the saddle to straddle his mount's rump, stretching the reins as he kicked his heels into its flanks.

He went down the slope with his horse wild-eyed and tossing its head. But its rear legs were dug in, slowing its progress. The girl followed, but by the time she reached the rocks by the zigzag course she had chosen, Reason had dismounted and floundered across the slope,

144

gasping when she saw the blood staining McCarty's face and torn jacket. He cried out in pain as Reason opened his jacket, took one look at the blood-sodden clothing beneath and closed it again. The deputy began to cough and bright crimson blood trickled from his mouth.

Reason shook his head at the girl's inquiring look. 'Ribs are all smashed. Must have penetrated his lungs.'

Annie made a mewling sound and slipped off her gloves, gently stroking McCarty's lacerated forehead. The deputy's eyes flickered open. They were clouded with pain and resignation as he looked up into the girl's face and tried to smile.

'Guess I'll never get to wear that – that sheriff's badge now, huh?' he said, straining for breath.

'Don't talk that way, Coop,' Annie told him, forcing a smile, but the truth was evident in her moist eyes and the catch in her voice. 'We will get you to Blall City. They have a fine infirmary there and good doctors …'

Cooper McCarty was already shaking his head slightly before she let the words trail off. He lifted a hand and feebly tugged at her jacket sleeve. 'Don't try to – f-fool me, Annie. I know I'm through.' He switched his pain-filled eyes to the drifter. 'Give it to me straight, Conant. I'm finished ain't I?'

The drifter looked away, hesitated, then looking back at the young deputy, nodded gently, putting out his hand to squeeze McCarty's shoulder lightly. 'You're kinda smashed up. Even if we managed to get you on a bronc, you would never make it to Blall City alive.'

Annie held back a sob as tears streaked down his cheeks. She wiped her eyes.

McCarty strained to speak, went into a fit of coughing

145

and wiping blood from his chin, turned a desperate face towards Reason. 'Get moving. Get the girl and that book to the marshal. Gimme my rifle and leave me in the rocks here. I-I will hold them off as long as I can.'

'No, we can't leave you here, Coop!' Annie protested tearfully.

Reason was already struggling up the slope to where the carcass of McCarty's mount lay. He worked the rifle out of the scabbard and took a box of shells from the saddlebags, but he didn't believe the deputy would be able to do much more than get off a couple of shots. He was too far gone.

Back amongst the rocks, he took the girl gently by the arm and helped her to her feet. 'Mount up, Annie. There is nothing else we can do for the deputy.'

'But he will be killed!' she protested.

Reason looked at her soberly. 'Likely be quicker and better than going the way he is now. You know there is nothing else we can do for him. He's as good as dead.'

She stared at him, wild-eyed and angry for a moment, then, choking back a sob, hurried towards her mount. Reason moved a rock to give Cooper a little more cover, levered a shell into the rifle's breech and put it in the injured man's hands.

'Sorry, Coop. You are a square shooter,' he said solemnly.

The deputy stared at him through a veil of pain and moved his blood-flecked lips in a crooked smile. 'You're pretty straight yourself, drifter,' he managed to say, his voice weak.

Reason squeezed his shoulder, went to his horse and swung into the saddle. The girl was still staring down at

McCarty, her cheeks wet, the tears beginning to freeze in the icy wind that swept up the slope. She started to speak but no words would come. The young deputy lifted a shaky hand in farewell as Reason Conant grabbed her mount's bridle and led it down the slope.

McCarty did not have enough strength left to turn his head and watch the other two leave. He was afraid the effort could send him plunging into unconsciousness.

If he had to die now, he wanted his death to be worth-while. He would go down fighting and give the drifter and the girl as much of a chance as possible to get them to Blall City ahead of the pursuing killers.

Gasping for breath during several fits of coughing, the deputy got the rifle against his shoulder as he mustered all the strength he could and sighted along the barrel, wondering just where on the ridge the group of killers would appear.

And silently hoping he lasted long enough to get a few shots at them.

Gideon Darrow, Ocie Kramer and Alonzo Conway were in such a hurry to finish this chore that when they did ride over the ridge, they were part way down the steep slope before they even spotted Cooper McCarty's dead horse.

The young deputy was barely conscious. He was fighting to stay awake, weakened by loss of blood and excruciating pain. His vision was rapidly going and the three pursuers were no more than blurs when he tried to line the rifle on them. The pain of his ribs brought him briefly back to full consciousness and his finger tight-ened on the trigger convulsively. The bullet ripped into the snow barely three yards in front of him.

It warned the others right off and instinctively they scattered, spreading out across the slope, guns coming up and raking McCarty's position with a volley of bullets as he was levering a fresh shell into the breech. The effort cost him dearly, for he went into a fit of violent coughing and his rifle exploded again, the lead hammering harmlessly into the snowbank in front of him.

Kramer was quick to sum up the situation. Two shots like that had to mean whoever was in charge of the gun was ailing mighty badly. With a yell he spurred his mount down towards the rocks, while Darrow and Conway stayed down in cover, believing the sheriff was out of his mind.

However, there was little risk involved for Kramer. McCarty thought to work the lever of his rifle but his fingers were too uncoordinated and he died that way, his hand locked through the lever of the rifle. The sheriff, riding into the clump of rocks, leant from the saddle, and emptied his pistol into the deputy's back. Then he viciously rode his mount across the blood-spattered body of the deputy, cursing McCarty, for he blamed the deputy for everything that had gone wrong. If Cooper McCarty had not returned to town when he had …

'That damned drifter and that blasted girl!' Darrow snapped as he rode down to join the sheriff, barely glancing at the dead deputy's body.

'I would say they rode straight down. In fact, if you look over this side of the rocks, you can see their tracks,' the sheriff explained.

'Yeah, I see them. Heading straight for Blall City!' exclaimed Conway, sounding more worried now than he had at any other time during the chase through the mountains. 'They cannot be that far ahead, can they?'

Ocie Kramer shook his head.

'Then let's move!' Gideon Darrow said emphatically. 'Even though we have got two men in town, I would rather take care of this out here and away from potential witnesses.'

The three men recklessly spurred down the slope.

CHAPTER 16

Reason Conant hipped in the saddle when he heard the gunfire and glanced quickly at the girl. She was awfully pale and tense.

'They are a lot closer than you thought, aren't they, Mr Conant?' Annie asked.

He hesitated, then nodded briefly. 'Must have made mighty good time ...' He paused as there was a rapid series of shots, then silence. His mouth tightened. 'That's it. A six-gun. They have nailed Coop. We don't have any time to lose, Annie.'

The girl was visibly upset, but at Reason's urging, spurred her mount, following him through a fold in the hills and up a trail that led to flat high country under the presence of the mountain's Shadow Peak, and the main trail into Blall City. The trouble was, they were still many miles away and could not hope to reach there by sundown.

Then Reason changed direction away and she called after him. 'The trail to town is not that way!'

'No, but this is safer! Kramer's no fool and those fellers have got plenty to lose. They could have a man watching that trail. We will have to cut across the hills. You know this high country?'

'Not too well, I'm afraid,' she told him.

'Well, long as we know the general direction of town and if we can hold them off until nightfall we might stand a chance,' Reason said as they galloped along a rocky trail that was relatively free of snow, allowing the weary horses to make better time.

But Kramer and Darrow knew this country well. Once they realized Reason and the girl had left the regular trail to Blall City, they guessed the drifter would instinctively head for the high ground. It was the logical thing to do.

'Maverick Mesa,' the sheriff said, riding his mount alongside Darrow's and pointing.

The miner nodded. 'That is where they will head for sure. You recollect that short cut through the old river course?'

Kramer grinned crookedly. 'Ought to. You and Alonzo keep following 'em and I will try and make it to the mesa ahead of them.'

The sheriff spurred his mount and headed away fast and, within minutes, he was in the midst of rocky ground with only sparse brush. Then, abruptly, he seemed to be swallowed up by the harsh country.

Conway's mouth fell open in surprise. 'What the hell ...'

Darrow laughed shortly. 'Old river bed, runs clear to the mesa – in fact, into the mesa. Once had its source underground, I guess, but dried up a ways back. Ocie chased an outlaw down there once, and caught him just as he was stashing his loot – gold I had sent down on the stage to Blall City. Officially, we never did find that gold, although the outlaw was caught and shot down by Kramer while trying to escape.'

'I never shared in that!' Alonzo Conway said instantly.

'It was before you come in with us,' Darrow told him shortly. 'Now spread out. Keep in the open and make sure that drifter can see us from the top of the mesa. With any luck, by the time he realizes there are only two riders coming, Ocie will be above him.'

Halfway up the winding trail leading to the mesa, Reason looked back to check on Annie, then beyond to the flats below. He felt grim satisfaction as he spotted the riders thundering through the juniper and sotol. He frowned when he saw only two riders and looked swiftly around for the third.

'Reason!'

The girl called suddenly and he whipped around again in time to see her leaping from her mount as the animal stumbled and floundered over the edge of the trail. The rim rock, brittle from the bitter cold, broke away under its hooves and it squealed in terror as it toppled over the edge and rolled down the slope. Annie was sprawled on all fours on the trail and Reason rode back to her.

She cowered away from the edge of the trail and Reason got his mount in front of her. He kicked his foot free of the stirrup, reached down for her hand and helped her up behind him.

'Let's hope my mount don't give up the ghost,' the drifter said as he urged it up the trail.

Reaching the top of the mesa, he reined in amongst

a nest of boulders, swung a leg over the saddle horn and jumped down. 'Climb down and stay here while I take a looksee.'

Crouching, he ran back to the trail and looked out over the flats.

There were still just two pursuers and they were closing in fast on the mesa trail. His mouth tightened: they had guessed he would make for the highest ground around to check the back trail, and he cursed himself for not having foreseen the possibility. He moved his gaze to the left and swore aloud when he saw a dry river course that cut clear across the flats and led right to the mesa itself. That meant the third man, riding hell for leather along the river bed, could now be on the mesa.

He spun and ran back to the rocks where he had left the girl.

Then he froze as he rounded the first of the big boulders and saw Ocie Kramer with one hand clamped over Annie's mouth. The cocked six-gun he held in his other hand was pointing straight at Reason Conant.

'What's the hurry, drifter?' the sheriff asked, grinning. 'You ain't got no place to go! 'Cept to hell!'

Reason swore under his breath and lifted his hands slightly.

'Try anything and I will blow her head off, drifter!' the sheriff warned grimly.

'Then you will never find the book,' Reason told him, throwing a warning glance at the girl as he saw her abruptly stop struggling and look at him in surprise. 'She is the only one who knows where it is.'

Kramer's eyes narrowed. He looked from Reason to the girl and shook her violently. 'That true, Annie?'

The girl hesitated and, still looking at Reason with fear-filled eyes, nodded briefly. She fought to pull the sheriff's glove down a little and Kramer eased the pressure enough for her to talk.

'I-I didn't know who I could really trust so I-I hid the book one night, while Cooper McCarty and Reason here were sleeping,' she gasped. 'But I won't tell you where it is, no matter what you do!'

Kramer laughed and clamped his hand over her mouth again. 'You wanna bet? Hell, it won't be no trouble at all to make you talk, Annie, and it will be pure pleasure to ask you the questions … Show you what I mean.' He laughed and his hand suddenly disappeared beneath her jacket. She sucked down a sharp breath.

Reason lunged forward, sweeping his jacket flap back, reaching for his gun and Kramer flung the girl aside, gun blasting. The bullet took Reason in the side and he spun away and crashed to the ground. The sheriff laughed again and placed his foot in the middle of Annie's chest as she struggled to sit up.

'See, all I gotta do is shoot the drifter to pieces a little at a time and you will tell me what I want to know,' the sheriff said devilishly.

Annie glanced at Reason's pain-contorted face, then she said, gulping, 'It-it's in the saddlebag on my horse. He fell over the edge of the trail.'

'Aw, hell,' Ocie Kramer said in genuine disappointment. 'I didn't want you to give up so easy, Annie! I wanted to have a chance to …'

Suddenly, from the corner of his eye, he caught a movement and swung around, but he wasn't fast enough.

Reason Conant spun onto his side, biting back the

agony it cost him, and his six-gun boomed twice. Kramer's gun roared too, but the lead hammered harmlessly into the ground as Reason's bullets smashed into the sheriff's chest. As the corrupt lawman dropped, Reason shot his again, then rolled to face the top of the trail at the sound of hoof beats.

'Get into the rocks!' he yelled to Annie as Darrow and Conway came thundering onto the mesa, shooting wildly.

Reason rolled onto his back and triggered a shot as Darrow rode his horse straight at him. The bullet thunked into the horse and it went down with Gideon Darrow sailing over its head. The drifter swung around, as Conway's gun roared, sending a bullet ploughing into the snow between his feet. He snapped two shots at the saloon keeper as he raced by on his mount and Conway yelled and threw up his arms as he was punched from the saddle. He hit hard and rolled against the rocks.

The drifter spun back towards Darrow who, shaken and bleeding from a cut on his forehead, had staggered to his feet and retrieved his gun which he had dropped in the fall. Reason triggered – but the hammer fell on an empty chamber.

Darrow bared his teeth as he straightened and wiped blood out of his eyes, his gun covering Reason. 'Well, well, well … drifter, end of the trail for you after all, huh? And you almost made it! Man, I could have used you. A feller like you would have had it made, but I know your stupid type. Got your codes and you stick to 'em. Fool.'

'I have bent the law on occasion, Mr Darrow,' Reason said, gritting his teeth against the pain in his side. 'Wide looped a few steers and so on, but not on the same scale as you. And I don't go in for corrupting politicians for profit. I reckon my code might not win me any medals, but I can live with my conscience. I reckon you don't have one, hiring scum to kill a good man like Annie's father.'

Darrow shrugged, glancing briefly at the girl. 'Clive was a fool. We offered to buy him off. Stupidly, he said no. Can you believe that? Codes, you see, drifter? And what did it get him but a bullet in the head? Same as it will get you, I'm afraid.'

'Gonna kill the girl too, Darrow? You will have a hard time explaining that away,' Reason countered.

The miner laughed. 'Hell no. I will rig it to make it look like you did it. They will think you managed to kill her before you and Kramer nailed each other.'

'The book!' Annie said suddenly. 'You are forgetting about the book!'

The miner shook his head. 'Heard you say it was in the saddlebag on your horse, which we saw on the way up. Doesn't really matter if it isn't. If you have hid it, no one will find it anyway, when you are dead. So …'

He lifted his pistol and lined it up on Reason's chest. The drifter steeled himself, wondering if he could scoop up a handful of gravel and toss it into Darrow's face before the hammer dropped.

'Run, Annie!' he yelled and scooped up the gravel, but there was a gunshot and he stiffened, hands only half closed around the stones.

He wondered why he didn't feel the bullet striking his big body. Then he saw Gideon Darrow sprawled on his face in the snow, blood staining the white snow, the back of his head blown off.

Reason looked up in surprise as a rider appeared over the rim of the mesa. It was Chet Young, clutching his smoking rifle and grinning sheepishly.

'Ma tore into me for leading that ugly feller, Powell, to you. She made me come after you to try and make it up to you,' he told them.

'Mighty glad you did, Chet,' Reason said, sitting up and examining the wound in his side. Then Annie Burch was beside him, her gentle fingers pushing his hands away. Her face was very close to his as she looked up.

'It's not serious, I am happy to say. But we better get you to Blall City before you lose too much blood. Will you lend me a hand please, Chet?' Annie asked.

After roughly bandaging Reason's wound and helping him into the saddle, Chet swung up onto his own mount and, with Annie riding Darrow's horse, they headed out.

'Was that book still in your saddlebag, by the way?' Reason asked Annie, as the three rode across the mesa.

She shook her head. 'Well, yes, it was – but the pages with the proof about the railroad land swindle were missing. I left them with Widow Young. She hid them in her coffee can.'

The drifter grinned. 'Well, they will nail the politicians and the railroad officials who were involved, too. Your father's efforts weren't for nothing after all, Annie.'

The young girl nodded soberly. 'Do you think Darrow might have men in Blall City waiting for us?'

'Maybe, but they won't move without his say so. They will just be there to observe, I reckon. And anyway, Chet will see we get to the marshal safely, huh, kid?'

Chet Young grinned and his chest swelled some.

'What will you do then?' Annie asked quietly. 'Move on?'

'Nope, I still need a job for the rest of winter, my

other attempts to secure income have failed. Don't aim to freeze my – well, to freeze, drifting around in the kind of weather you got in these parts,' Reason replied.

Annie smiled suddenly. 'Know anything about running a newspaper?'

'Hell, no! I'm a cowhand.'

'It's warmer than riding the range – and I could teach you,' she said with a smile.

He rode in silence for a time, then said quietly, 'Well, now, that makes the offer sound a whole lot better. A whole lot better.'

Annie's smile widened. It was answer enough for her.